MANY
ME
TOO

PREMA HARISHANKAR

LifeRich Publishing is a registered trademark of The Reader's Digest Association, Inc.

LifeRich Publishing books may be ordered through booksellers or by contacting:

LifeRich Publishing
1663 Liberty Drive
Bloomington, IN 47403
www.liferichpublishing.com
1 (888) 238-8637

ISBN: 978-1-4897-2434-2 (sc)
ISBN: 978-1-4897-2433-5 (hc)
ISBN: 978-1-4897-2435-9 (e)

Library of Congress Control Number: 2019910947

Print information available on the last page.

LifeRich Publishing rev. date: 10/24/2019

CONTENTS

PREFACE

The #Me Too movement encouraged us to get the truth out in the open. These stories deserve to come out, because not doing so will be detrimental to the moral progress of human race. That it's deserved is evident from the stories we hear. Growing up in India as a young girl, I witnessed violations all around me. They ranged from very subtle verbal abuses to outrageous plots to silence women. The daily distractions of life got us away from the potency of problems proving people can get used to anything! All incidents eventually blurred into an avalanche of social dreadfulness which left a lingering repulsiveness.

The Novella, "Vainglorious Lout" provides an insight into the life of a mortal describing himself as an all-knowing mentor; he habitually puts women down in his orations and damages the lives of everyone around him. This short-story deals with various aspects of a society where brilliant and humble men fail to identify their counterparts possessing exaggerated ideas of themselves.

A couple of college students go through 'Many Me Too' experiences of inappropriate touching on their daily commute to their university. Their discussions reveal the deterrents they could put in place to make their short trip to their learning centers, peaceful.

"No Escape" does not fall under #Me Too; it shows an everyday hero, a very sensible young man who is interested in the welfare of his family of two younger sisters. Good men in this world are plentiful.

A middle-aged stalker gets to be noticed promptly and 'risk mitigation' is put in place like a stitch in time to save his face and his family members from shame. Stalking comes in various sizes. Even in its simplest form, it can be terrifying.

Work-place behaviors of inappropriateness follow a pattern that are discernable. It happens to the detriment of its regular players; but damages that happen in different societies are not readily understandable; hence this book. The international acceptance and stronghold of #Me Too, in itself, reiterate the notion that the issues are universal.

Vainglorious Lout

CHAPTER 1

The other man I had dreamed
A drunken, vainglorious lout.
He had done most bitter wrong
To some who are near my heart,
Yet I number him in the song.

— "Easter 1916," William Butler Yeats (1865–1939)

Emails came flying in asking SriSham to cancel the prayer session on the second Saturday of August 2017; everyone was worried about Hurricane Harvey.

"Oh, no need to cancel the class. Things will be fine. Our saint is here to take care of you and me. I am here too, am I not?"

The host said, "We can make it a session where we could say a prayer for Harvey not to damage Houston and other Texas areas as they have predicted it will."

SriSham freaked out. Harvey was not going to ruin his favorite day. He replied coolly but firmly, "The class and the prayer session are not cancelled. No reason to conduct a special session for Harvey. It will be a regular session." And that was that.

SriSham had come to look forward to the second Saturdays of every month. He recorded the rich TV evangelists' shows and listened to them constantly. He pictured the YouTube videos of all the Hindu mentors, in his mind as though he had written them. He knew the speeches of all renowned Indian and Christian leaders past and present like the back of his hand. He was about sixty-eight and retired; he sat all day in front of his computer answering questions from devotees and watching YouTube.

He started his discourse with a question: "Has anyone here felt the power of this saint?"

Vivek, sitting in the front row, said, "I have, because I have received accolades from you for the past ten years."

"That's right," SriSham said. "Once you feel his presence, there's nothing to fear except fear itself. These prayer sessions with me get immediate results. This saint belongs to this country, a country of instant gratification. Harvey will be subdued instantaneously just like this man seated here found his lost inhaler. He found it in thirty minutes, and it happened in this home." He sounded as if he walked on water.

"Wait a minute, sir," the bold nine-year-old son of the host asked from the front row, "did you just compare Harvey to finding lost knick-knacks?"

"Yes." SriSham had to stick to his declarations. "But you cannot take my statements literally. After all, our saint is unfathomable, and his ways are unknowable. We will see each other at our next prayer session on September ninth. Only my devotees have this ability to come out of catastrophes unscathed. This saint is known to control the elements. He once stopped a tornado from obliterating the Baylor College of Medicine by making it turn ninety degrees. The weather experts had no idea how that had happened. But the previous evening, Baylor College students had called me to their rescue: 'Sri sir, our medical labs and classrooms will be obliterated. Sir, please do something,' I replied, 'I have already done something.' Troy Dungan came on the nine o'clock news and said, 'Never in my twenty-five years of being a weather expert have I known a tornado to change its path in the last minute and spared a great city.' The next day, all the students came and met me to thank me."

That was the last straw for the host's son. He stood and asked, "Are you saying you will stop Harvey in its tracks and Houston will escape this time?" Even his parents were not shushing him. What stood in front of them was a gigantesque Brobdingnagian storm.

SriSham could have easily said, "No, all I'm saying is that no damage will come to my devotees' homes or lives" or something to that effect. Most of his devotees lived north of Houston in mansions; none lived in low-lying areas or near the eye of the storm where it was supposed to make landfall. Instead, he blurted out, "Yes! I'm saying that Harvey will go away like a scaredy-cat without touching Houston or any other part of Texas. In fact, it will die at sea."

"I challenge you to go the beach and stay there on the day it's supposed to land."

With appropriate seriousness, SriSham accepted the challenge. It was important for him to win over this younger crowd, this second generation of Indian boys. After all, Houston had never seen the likes of Harvey that the weather anchors and meteorologists were predicting it would be.

"Young man, you have piqued my desire to stop this storm completely. Yes, Harvey will not come anywhere near Houston. I will stop it far, far away from land with the help of our saint."

SriSham looked at the saint's picture. "Let us continue to report about Harvey and its death in the seas in our next class." SriSham took the challenge lightly and continued his discourse.

He seemed somewhat angry and restless for the rest of his discourse. He blamed the CEO of IBM for their connections not working properly when a devotee said his last class's audio was not clear. "No wonder—IBM is headed by a woman," SriSham pronounced loudly. "But no worries. I will tell Mr. Pi about this. He can easily resolve it. He was in great trouble last month, Google was, but he should be just fine. He consults me regularly."

He saw some newcomers entering just then for the food hoping that the prayer session was over. SriSham commanded them to come to the prayer session before food. "This is for the newcomers only—pray for just one minute. Be in the presence of this great saint, who is alive in this picture, and close your eyes. Our saint says you will get everything you want in your life, and who am I to question his ways? After all, they are enigmatic and perplexing."

That discourse was extremely succinct; he seemed to have been truly distracted. He tried to remain very calm and thoughtful while devotees queued up to fall at his feet or touch his feet. He handed out the bags of flower petals and drove home with Rashmi.

On Thursday, August 24, 2017, SriSham left for Galveston, about forty miles south of Houston. He had never been to the beach though his daughter loved it. Since his days as a disciple of his saint, SriSham has been a hero for the first generation of Indian immigrants in Houston, but the younger generation seemed to elude him. He planned to make an example of his powers by taming Harvey. Performing such a deed would force them to accept him or at least keep their disparaging comments at bay. There might not be a better opportunity to show them his power. He considered himself predestined to survive the heat he was taking.

As he drew closer, he discovered that more and more roads were blocked. SriSham was pulled over by an emergency crew. "Sir, where are you headed? Didn't you see the signs? The road's closed ahead," a man yelled over the wind and rain. The down-pour had started already.

SriSham disliked authority. "I am headed to the beach to pray for the storm not to reach Houston."

"Sir, the governor preemptively declared a state of disaster. It's in your best interest to dutifully turn around and go home. The rain will be torrential soon."

"Officer, the track of the storm is not very certain. Didn't meteorologist Reilly say so? The prayer I am going to say will make sure Harvey doesn't come anywhere near Houston or in fact not land anywhere but die in the sea. Officer, I'm determined to stay at least here if not reach the beach."

"Sir, if you don't heed the warnings, I have the authority to arrest you and keep you in the precinct until someone can actually come in this deluge to take you home."

"Officer, my prayer is for the protection and deliverance of Houston from Harvey's wrath!"

The emergency crew looked askance at the offer of this saffron-clad swami. They radioed in for help, and in a short while, two policemen arrested SriSham and took him to the nearby police station.

SriSham had high hopes as he watched the TV in the police station. Niki Bender, the emergency management coordinator for Galveston, came on TV and assured viewers that the track of the storm was very uncertain; that gave SriSham hope of surviving his promise.

But on Friday, August 25th night around ten, it happened. Harvey made landfall and tore up the shore and shattered people's hopes. Relentless devastation engulfed the great Lone Star State. Harvey behaved worse than expected.

CHAPTER 2

It was many moons before Harvey and a second Saturday of the month. SriSham entered the foyer. Men, women, and a few children stood reverentially on both sides of the two-story foyer of the grand, new, multimillion-dollar home in a suburb of Houston. It was wide open and decorated in creamy lacquer. It had thronged with activity until this Pecksniffian person stepped in.

There were about thirty-five of them, two-thirds being women. All of them had flowers reduced to petals, sepals, stamens, and pistils in their palms. As SriSham crossed the foyer, the patrons came slightly closer to the revered man and showered his feet with the blossoms. SriSham was amused and pleased. He was in fact speechless. Slowly progressing down the hallway, he appeared at the entry of what looked like the family room.

SriSham looked about fifty though he was sixty-six. He was tall and lanky and could have been handsome but for the slight stoop of his shoulders. His fine lineament made him the image of his mother.

Before moving all the way into the room and taking the seat that was ready for him, he turned stealthily to look at the foyer, where the women were collecting the petals he had trampled on. They bagged them by hand in their extended saris or scarves or shirt tails. As they did so, most closed their eyes, muttered something, and pressed the petals to one and then the other closed eye. The women repeated the action a few times, and SriSham noticed that some men did the same.

A meek request came from the host of the house: "All of you, please come in."

People glided into the family room, and polite and hushed conversation ensued; everyone was smiling broadly. No one sat. SriSham looked at the place that had been readied for him—a cushioned chair, a table in front on which lay a big silver punch bowl brimming with freshly cut flowers, a table lamp for him to use while referring to his speech notecards, and a small fan. *Ah, just as it has always been as before*, he thought. This was a relief to SriSham, and yes, the preparations were immaculate.

In the next few hours, the table would bear numerous sheets of paper, pens, pencils, and Lysol disinfecting wipes all hiding the table with endless teacup marks. In the bare areas, there were plastic containers of oil, binder clips in odd colors, sizes, and shapes to secure his shawl in place, and dollar bills to reward children who answered questions correctly.

SriSham waited for others to converse with him, but they were too polite to open their mouths first. Some of them stood with stiff, folded hands clasped in front, palms hugging one another, or hands in pants pockets. They gazed at SriSham or at a picture on the wall. There were a few Caucasians, but most of them were Indian immigrants who had been living in the United States for a couple of decades or more. He called them ten-dollar millionaires; they boasted of having come to the United States with very little and had become millionaires in a few decades. Most of them were middle-aged fathers and mothers who had not acquired the habit of going out on Saturday evenings with family and friends; they had left India in the nineties and were not used to the drinking or pub-going culture.

Some of them had planned to go back to India for good after five years of earning and saving money, but they had extended their stay to eight years, fifteen years, thirty years. Having one leg in India and the other in the United States had stretched them out of shape and had left them unable to assimilate well. Those who did visit India came back with stories of the crowds, the water's scarcity and poor quality, and constant sickness due to pollution.

A general awkwardness prevailed in the crowd.

"Guruji, would you like a cup of coffee or tea?" asked Soori, the man of the house. He stood at a respectful distance from SriSham but close enough to be heard. He bent slightly at the waist in SriSham's direction and waited for SriSham's response.

"Just hot water please," SriSham said with a forced smile. He glanced at Soori's wife, who was standing at the head of the cluster of wives who were separate from their spouses and keenly observing the conversation between her better half and the grand guest of the evening ready to peel away and run to the kitchen.

Soori announced generally to the crowd of women, "Please get some hot water in a kettle and a tumbler." His wife nodded, and two or three sari-clad aunts headed to the stove.

After a few minutes, the conversation in the family room was slowly getting started. Soori's wife came with a kettle and silver tumbler; it was customary in India to use only the best silver utensils for the higher-ups.

SriSham stood, took a few sips, and set the tumbler on the table in front of his chair. "Correct temperature," he said in the direction of the woman. "This would have been a treat a few months ago on my cold Himalayan trek. Thank you."

He smiled at Soori's wife, which caused her to blush and return the smile. As the hot water got into his system, his thoughts turned to the trekking paths on which he had successfully lost his second wife as they were trudging around Mount Kailash from the grand and pristine Lake Manasarovar.

SriSham and his group had flown from Houston Hobby toward the end of April 2017. They were to start their sojourn around Kailash the first week of May; they allowed for delays due to bad weather. There were only about ten in the group. He had given them exact instructions for their baggage—one backpack for trekking and one piece of hand luggage that contained a sleeping bag, a warm change of clothes, and an extra pair of shoes.

They had landed in Kathmandu, Nepal, after one stop in

Dubai. His wife, Nirmala, was sick from the journey, or so he said, from Houston to Kathmandu and weak due to the fasting she had undertaken for months before the trip. SriSham had been quite stringent with her and had asked her to practice a daily regimen of self-mortification that included fasting every night, sacrificing dinner, praying many times a day, and sleeping on the floor. That was the only way the fairer sex could go to Kailash without incurring the wrath of Shiva he had decreed.

Nirmala knew no other way of getting there without his blessing. The cost was astronomical, and SriSham banned her from the company of anyone other than himself. This intelligent woman had seen no way of getting there without SriSham and so had gone along with his requests. She dared not speak to SriSham about the other women who had been to Mount Kailash without having performed any penances. She had seen many a picture of matrons in Kailash and heard their stories about their Kailash sojourns firsthand; she knew very well it involved no fasting or penance.

SriSham had expected her to last until Kathmandu and had planned mentally on an open cremation at the Pashupathinath Temple as was common and customary. But he was surprised that she was only drifting in and out until they had reached Nepalgunj and later Simikot. She was very alive and strong at heart but feeling lonely and looking pained.

"I want to die in Kailash because I don't want to be born again," she kept muttering as they boarded the helicopter from Simikot.

By the time they reached Lake Manasarover, all she had left was a heart that was beating slowly. "Oh, it's the height and the oxygen supply," SriSham said nonchalantly.

As they reached the great Lake Manasarovar, Nirmala was excited; he had her drink directly from the lake since as he told her it was the lake that the holiest of spirits drank from every day. As he expected, Nirmala developed diarrhea and incessant vomiting.

She continued her fasting as per his instructions since it was after all a trip to the god's abode. Her condition worsened as the day proceeded to night, and then SriSham declared to his group, "Nirmala will stay here if she wants, and I will stay with her. At the break of dawn tomorrow, all of you should start out."

Around five the next morning, he woke them up and told them to take a dip in the lake and get ready to leave.

"Go straight to the gate, Yamadhwara, the place where the path starts to go around Kailash. My wife wants a horse, and I will bring her slowly on horseback. I am not going to delay you on our behalf. Having come all the way from the United States, she is not going back without going around the holy mountain, right? We'll catch up back here maybe in four or five days."

SriSham hired a horse to carry his wife around Mount Kailash; the owner insisted that he take a Sherpa with him. SriSham vehemently denied the mandate because he was a seasoned traveler who had visited Kailash with a group at least once a year for some time. He proceeded by himself with Nirmala on the horse. He was the leader of the group; they did not stop him. The locals had seen him being revered and had come to touch his feet on several occasions. So SriSham did not have to argue—he got his horse sans Sherpa.

Nirmala sat on the horse that SriSham led; the group had gone ahead. He was falling behind everyone and every group, and as the sun was setting, she was bent over on the horse in a sleeping posture. Her hands held onto the reins feebly as SriSham's hand supported her. In a little while, he stopped the horse and slowly got her off. He laid her on the ground. He pressed a pillow to her face. Not having eaten properly for months and weakened by the diarrhea attacks, she did not put up much of a fight.

The rest, though, was not as easy as SriSham had envisioned. Problems unfolded one by one and not without drama, a lot of drudgery, and many dollars. He had planned to go back to the camp at Lake Manasarover without alerting his crew and arrange for a helicopter to fly her body and him to Kathmandu that night.

However, the weather did not cooperate. He was forced to stay with her mortal remains for almost a day before lifting off after having spent a hefty amount due to emergency. Keeping her body in the morgue of a slovenly hospital in Kathmandu came at an exorbitant price as well; he arranged to have her cremated the next day. Open cremations at Pashupatinath Temple were only too common, so he had no problems attaining permission from the temple as he was a respected citizen of the United States and a well-known god-man among the New Delhi families who were his followers. By the time the rest of the group met him back in Kathmandu, the cremation had taken place.

SriSham's bewitched and gripping account fascinated his followers. He tried to console his spellbound crew: "She got exactly what she wanted—to die in Kailash in the lap of Shiva and be cremated at Pashupatinath Temple overlooking the holiest of rivers, the Bagmati, ultimately to join hands with the Ganges River."

He beckoned them to board the plane as per their schedule and go back to Houston; he was going to travel to the southern parts of India to perform final rites for his wife in well-known temples where his wife had been a regular in her younger days and would return to Houston in a month or so.

He got lost in parts of India where no one knew him. He regularly watched all the US news channels and was in touch with Emma, his ardent devotee, to feel the pulse of the thirty-some families in Houston who had invited him at least once for what he called discourses.

Someone in the suburban home intruded on his thoughts and brought SriSham back to his forbidding self with a mundane question: "How was the trip to Mount Kailash, Guruji?" The question was asked politely, but SriSham felt terribly irritated. Without showing it to the crowd that was paying for his daily bread and butter, he gave a broad but sad smile; kindness emanated from his eyes.

Another voice erupted from the small crowd: "Sorry for your loss." That came from a man standing next to the first. He spoke loudly as he pushed the first one away from SriSham. *The first one may not have known of the tragedy*, SriSham thought with some relief.

The second man obstinately came forward and gave his condolences again. Noticing the first man's puzzled look, SriSham answered politely, "Yes, it was her time to go, and she was very peaceful to leave her body on Mount Kailash you know. That's all she had ever wanted all her life, and I suppose she is one of the luckier ones in that she received what she had wanted," SriSham replied with a gasp.

Others came forward and stood by the second man listening attentively to SriSham. A question came from the women's side: "How does one achieve what he or she wants?"

SriSham turned around trying to control his excitement at hearing a familiar voice. He gave the gorgeous Emma a lascivious look as she came close to him in her colorful ethnic outfit. She was in her early forties, but she looked ten years younger due to thoughtful dieting and exercise. The gym rat that she was, her face radiated persuasiveness. She had a wide, somewhat naughty, and very contagious smile. Long strands of jasmine hung parallel to her braid as was the case with other women there, but Emma did not wear much jewelry in contrast to the other women. She had a camera in her hands; she was the photographer for the group, and she was there on a job, a mission—to bring SriSham into the limelight.

Emma recited to herself lines of the bard in "As You Like It": "Even now, as I commence my task, his full-toned voice swells in my ears; his lustrous eyes dwell on me with all their melancholy sweetness."

"Easy," SriSham said with a smile. He was happy and relieved to change the subject back to familiar territory. "If you attend this prayer session we have every second Saturday of the month and chant his name"—he pointed to a large, framed photograph of a thin, elderly man clad in saffron clothes seated on the floor with his legs crossed, palms resting on his knees, and eyes closed — "you can achieve anything you want." SriSham dramatically closed his eyes in what seemed like prayer. All questioners stopped at this deliberate sign. The crowd stepped back.

He opened his eyes that were swelling with tears and said slowly, "It is not enough that you see him in me." But no one had ever told SriSham that they had ever seen the saint in the photo in him. "You should see him in everyone. That is the only way to achieve inner peace. This is the most powerful prayer and celebration one can have on earth that produces the desired effect. The young boys here will grow up to be senators, and the girls will go to Harvard Medical School if you attend this prayer at least once every month."

He knew exactly what to say to a crowd of middle-aged, first-generation Indian fellows and their female counterparts, who wore iridescent saris and bold necklaces; they were demure and acquiescent to their gentlemen.

SriSham had an uncanny resemblance to the man in the photograph. Though he knew very well that that was just coincidence, it seemed to influence his current predicament. SriSham's late mother had had extremely fair skin for a woman of Indian descent and was very slender and small boned. He had acquired his mother's complexion and build, which were similar to those of the man in the picture. Though no one had ever said anything about their resemblance, SriSham would bring it up as if it were the one ace he held. SriSham always made a point of telling everyone that the man in the photograph was he in his earlier birth and hence the physical resemblance.

"Sit down please, all of you," the hostess asked her guests, but everyone kept standing; SriSham knew they would not sit until he took his seat, but he wanted to put that to a test, so he kept standing, and the people obediently stood looking intently at him.

The host came over to SriSham and said, "Sir, please take your seat, sir." SriSham did. The crowd performed wholesome obeisance by folding their palms on their chests and bowing to the seated

SriSham before sitting on the carpeted floor. To his utter relief and peace, he realized that his two months' stay in India after his wife's supposedly unfortunate death had not changed the crowd there in Houston—not an iota.

The craziness of holding a god-man in high esteem and making him theirs early in the game had taken over the minds of some highly educated and financially successful folks in the US. They were looking for ways to manage their stress and get on the bandwagon early before the god-man became too famous or too rich to catch. Giving small amounts of money to support a god-man bought big amounts of happiness, and they derived strength by belonging to a group. The cult of personality particular to India made heroes of stars in films, sports, and politics in addition to religion.

None in the Houston group was religious in the traditional sense; they did not read the Bhagavad Gita or Ramayana; it was ironic that SriSham did not know Sanskrit either. He had learned that it was easier to con nonreligious rich men than it was to con poor but learned men. The tech workers in his group were not the praying type. They tried to create a compact mass; when someone skipped an event, SriSham sent them on guilt trips. He called those who deserted a dialogue rats. He created fear in the hearts of latecomers by accusing them of losing sight of their goals or being stoned while driving; the behemothian difference being that there were no drugs or ashrams or extortions. This god-man said that this was about their future; he told them he could tell five hundred years of their lives from that day on including their next births.

SriSham checked the mic and cleared his throat. He waited for the chatter to die down. When he started speaking, the crowd fell silent.

"Today's topic is very relevant to what happened on the trails in the Himalayas a few months ago. The importance of a spouse to men and women of this planet"—he gestured grandiloquently to those gathered—"the deep penetration with which a man goes into a woman's heart"—he stealthily looked at Emma without the crowd noticing but noticed that a young man seated on the stairwell was chuckling—"the love of a man and a woman in a marriage should give boundless happiness to each other." The woman seated in the front row to his side gave off a forlorn look that SriSham did not miss.

The crowd enjoyed his ramblings and musings, and God knows SriSham himself loved to listen to himself. After all, he was their talisman that would give them notable futures; he was received with intense respect by this crowd. *And why not?* he asked himself rhetorically. He had come to value his loquaciousness, his bread and butter. Too bad he did not have a funny bone, but he made it up by instilling fear in the crowd; he told them that those who did not heed him would die in terrible accidents. Those who spoke ill of his prayer sessions would get throat cancer and untold other miseries, but those who were obedient would find that their children would enjoy brilliant professional careers.

Theosophists came from East and are continuing to come to touch and change many lives for the good. They talk about the frailty of life and its transitoriness. Their contributions and the impact they create are under the workings of the mind and the inner-self. They help to stay fit and teach to meditate for peace. The good ones presented that the best ways to serve God was through serving mankind. The true Master had huge following. They were also financially very successful.

SriSham was different from them all.

SriSham took his seat, and the harangue shifted to his devotees that he insisted were online listening to him. "I thank the technology team for enabling all the connection throughout this planet." The technology team he referred to consisted of Soori, and Emma. There were generally a few listeners—one family in Atlanta, a single man in Dallas, a couple in Austin, and a newcomer from San Diego. Emma showed up in the host's home, called the families confirming their availability, and connected them online. It took her just twenty minutes before a meeting to establish connections with them.

That day, just the elderly Austin couple was listening in. SriSham preferred to address each of them as a center; one by one, he elaborated the cities and their names including their pets' names if they had any.

Emma deliberately did not make it clear to him that just one family was online for fear of insulting SriSham.

"Devotees listening in Austin, Washington, Atlanta, and San Jose, welcome to this congregation. This huge turnout is very heartwarming." He had the habit of addressing his thirty or forty listeners as a congregation and closely followed the sermon style of popular TV evangelists. He watched TV for several hours before coming to one of these sessions; he took notes and reveled in them in front of a mirror mimicking the voice, tone, texture, and sometimes even the content of what he heard.

He mentioned all of the centers again but added a few more that time: "As I welcome my devotees from the centers of Houston, Austin, Atlanta, and San Jose, I am not forgetting to invite the center in Switzerland, which has just connected. Mr. Sandhu, who left on vacation with his family last week, has now joined us. It must be the wee hours of the morning there. I asked him to go to bed, but he wouldn't listen, and so he is awake at one in the morning to listen. And let's not forget the centers in India, where they are awake at this ghastly hour of four thirty in the morning."

SriSham finished with an ego-ridden, proud smile hoping or imagining his ex-brother-in-law, a surgeon, was keenly listening in.

The innocent host stood there confused knowing he had not made connections to Switzerland or India; when he asked Emma about that later, she told him firmly that she had.

"You all must know Kannan, my Atlanta devotee," SriSham continued. Nobody knew such a devotee, but SriSham did not care. "He did not call me for a few months, and suddenly this morning, he called"—he continued with a bit of bitterness— "and said, 'Dear Guruji, I am tired of this waiting game. I am not getting a permanent position in the research lab that I have been working for the past two years to get.' My answer to him was, 'Well, you thought of your master only when you did not get something you wanted. If you had had the discourse at your place when I could come to Atlanta or at least had been in touch with me, you would have been a permanent employee by now.'"

SriSham did not make it clear whether he was referring to himself or to the saint in the photo. The ambiguity was purposeful. He sometimes referred to the person in the photo on the wall as the master, but the phone calls, emails, questions, and answers were to be sent to him to be honored by their master, and SriSham answered them. He kept his devotees in perpetual confusion on this matter.

"There's a lot of scientific evidence for this answer of mine, which is nothing but a matter of cause and effect. If anyone wants to challenge me on this, please come forward, take my seat, and give today's oration replacing me, but Prime Minister Modi will not like it for sure." He stopped and enjoyed the puzzled look on their faces. Someone timidly asked, "Is Prime Minister Modi listening to this lecture?"

"Prime Minister Modi's personal strategist and I are working on a project to improve India's plight. That was the main reason for my delay in coming back to the United States after my Kailash sojourn." Such preambles always worked. "Thank you for the large turnout," he said in spite of the fact there were only thirty there. "I tell you, after seeing these young minds here in this congregation, for which their karma has to be thanked, I am going to bless them."

SriSham made a loose fist using his right palm thus forming a tunnel and vigorously blew three times through the small opening surrounded by his thumb and fingers as if he were blowing into a breathalyzer at the behest of a cop. "You can catch those breaths," he said condescendingly. All devotees dutifully caught something in the air, raising their right hands, and placed their catch on their heads. Some of the youths acted as if they were catching his breaths and putting them on their heads, as well.

SriSham had set a plastic food container with a lid on the table to his left; it contained what seemed like fine clear oil. He asked his devotees to stop by the table after his lecture and receive a drop of the oil he had collected from all the temples of their saint in India. "This oil is capable of curing every malady in every single part of the body mentioned in *Grey's Anatomy* and more," he told them.

"I would normally ask you to keep the oil in front of our saint's picture near the altar at your home. Now here's a twist, an even better and faster way to health benefits, which I heard from my conversations with our saint. Guess what? You can mix this oil with the lilies and tulips that you will be so lucky to receive from me after this prayer session. Put the oil and flowers in a pail of water. Drink the water first thing in the morning and your health will be on cloud nine. You have not been asked to do this before, so you do not know the results, but start doing this tomorrow morning, and when we meet three Saturdays from today, every one of you will be narrating your success stories!"

Illnesses that confounded medical experts cured with his oil… the young fellow seated on the stairs was clenching his abdomen trying hard to suppress his laughter.

SriSham's attention turned to the picture on the altar. "This is a beautiful picture of our saint. This is the most beautiful picture I have ever seen. It's most exquisite due solely to the devotion and dedication of our hostess. Without such love, a picture in your home can never look this amazing."

SriSham always made it a point to shower extraordinary praises on his hosts and hostesses and their children. That often prompted them to host future prayer sessions when no one else had offered to host one of his dialogues. "Our saint leaves a twenty-four-karat gold coin underneath his image for such ardently dedicated piety. He will stick his hand out the photograph and leave the coin for the hostess—such is the power of his penetration." SriSham is going to charter the water, since Emma's presence made him happy. SriSham, at that point wanted to get a glimpse of Emma's reaction at his last word, but the boy in the stairwell looked suspiciously at Emma as SriSham pronounced the last word, hence not allowing his will.

"I know every devotee here who put the garlands together and who cooked what items. Thank you all. Let us now jump into the lecture. You have all heard my lectures of course on several occasions, but you have not read my books because they are still half-done. These are all real stories. I have so many examples of this man playing around, moving you like marbles on a Chinese checkers board. How do you beseech Him?"

He stopped for a moment and dramatically raised his voice. "For the senior badminton player among us, Amrith, who is here today, our saint will help him ace his game. His thrust is going to be remarkable." Obviously, SriSham missed company during the two months he had spent in India. "Do you all know the best badminton players in history?" The crowd fell quiet. A great memory was one of SriSham's strengths; he knew all the winners and remembered their names once he heard them. "Gao Ling of China, Kim Dong-Moon of South Korea, and Taufik Hidayat of West Java." SriSham gave a victorious smile. "Our Amrith will become the next Mr. Ling."

Amrith became shy as people turned to look at him. Amrith had moved to a new home in a fifty-five-plus community, where elderly adults played shuttlecock for exercise.

"Our saint always blesses us with nothing but the best. If Shashi wants to become the CEO of her company, she will have to have the willpower to do just that"

The gathering turned to Shashi, who was seated in the front row. She had been a homemaker until a few months ago. She had an eight-year-old and a five-year-old and had become an insurance agent when they started school because she was bored at home, and she had told SriSham that.

"But then, they are blessed incessantly by their guru." SriSham again was teasing them about who blessed them; was it the saint in the picture or his deputy sitting in front of them?

"All of us know that there's an easy path for us to victory, whatever that might mean for you ... and you ... and you," SriSham said while pointing at a few in the crowd. "And that is to attend this second-Saturday *sathsang*, which is communion with truth or in the company of truth. And there's a delicious seven-course dinner at the end of it.

"In only a few years, all of you will meet with success after success. I am aware of the deep karma of all of you when you say you do not have time to come to this prayer session for my counsel. I want to tell you that many moons ago, about 2000 years ago, I wrote a beautiful poem in which I said unless one touches this master's feet"—he pointed to the photo on the wall— "which everyone cannot comprehend, it is very difficult for you to get rid of your job anxieties. Your bad karma of past births may stop you from walking toward our saint, I mean, attending my lectures. But your constant true anxiety should be about finding a way and time to come to these sessions.

"You may ask if this is the only way to reach him. My answer to that question is a resounding 'yes'. I am here, am I not? Come to me, and I will teach you how to reach his feet. I am bringing all humanity to this incomparable one. Even Martians will one day march toward him. After that, Jupiter will barter with our saint's minister. Mercury will get the luxury of this watery planet's exemplary saint. Venus will focus on the precious and gracious us. Wanton Saturn will fashion its functions after our patron saint. Our saint is the ruling czar of our star. From alphabets to planets, he has them in his pocket."

Throughout the discourse, SriSham shot leering, oblique glances at Emma. She was moving about taking photos of the crowd from different angles and occasionally resting and being attentive to his speech.

This effulgent creator needed to appeal to the value-driven crowd too; So, he taught that only when the intellect was connected to wisdom could an intellectual distance be achieved, and that consciousness was the locus of the intellect. He had them mulling over what he narrated.

"When my devotees go to hospitals for surgeries, I am in touch with their surgeons. I am in the operating room visible only to the devotee. The devotee may be the patient lying on the operating table, or he may be the surgeon himself, in which case I will be giving power to him and instructions as well, if he needs them, to make the operation a success. My surgeon devotee was astonished not knowing I was moonlighting in his Houston hospital." SriSham chuckled.

"I safeguard the planes my devotees are on. I always tell my devotees that I will be present on all the flights they take. I am better than the air marshals because they are there only on a select few flights, but I am there on every one of the winged chariots even if there's just one devotee in the entire plane be it a jumbo jet or a small propeller plane, a thirty-seater. If there's an empty seat, I may even occupy it physically. You may think I am also traveling somewhere in the same plane, but I will be visible only to you."

For some reason, he did not say he would have bothered the pilot. SriSham seemed to have been enamored only of surgeons.

The young fellow on the stairwell asked, "Sir, won't you indulge the pilots?" That was a pithy observation to which SriSham's retorted, "No questions during the discourse. I will be the only one addressing and asking questions. You should be answering my questions, not the other way around. I am beyond all questioning at this point," SriSham answered seriously. He did not seem to have paid attention to the young man's question, or he may have understood it but was too fragile to answer a question seeping in ridicule. The young fellow's mother promptly called his name and requested him to be quiet.

SriSham continued with a story to acquaint the young boy and the crowd with his omnipotence. Every time someone questioned his stories, the stories that followed were mind-blowing. In that tradition, SriSham quickly came up with this one.

"When I was coming back from my India trip, there was this white American, I mean a Caucasian, seated next to me. I could tell that his consciousness level was nine, just like mine. As I have enlightened my devotees before, not everybody gets to be on consciousness level eight or nine, just a handful on this planet. Most of you are on level three or four mainly because your karmic evolution brought me to your presence. It would be lower than three if not for my presence.

"I said I am on the cusp of eight and nine because I was in the presence of our saint for the last seven births. At Harvard University, they proved these conscientious levels of human beings. In fact, I can make it clearer to you right away. Are there any neurosurgeons in the congregation?"

Everyone looked around to see if any hands went up from the floor.

"Okay, today there's none. Oh well, are there any neuroscientists here?"

SriSham would accept the next best if not the best. The crowd looked around again, and there was none.

"That's fine. Let me familiarize you with the fact that all of us are on very different consciousness levels. One look at each of you and I can tell your consciousness level. In fact, I have asked my daughter to study neuroscience and consciousness levels in Harvard, the prestigious institution she will be attending soon. When you are on level eight or higher, as I am, you can see several of your and others' future and past births. In fact, you will be timeless. You will be timeless, like me – I have no past or future" (The young man on the stairwell completed SriSham's sentence feebly to himself -*no future for sure*).

"In fact, let me, I will myself prove these consciousness levels scientifically. I am sure all of you have studied about the non-compressibility of water. If you immerse a small cup into a bucket of water and draw the cup out, the water in the cup will measure only up to a cup. But, if you took a one-gallon jar into a bucket of water and immersed it in water, when you draw the gallon jug out, that container could have drawn one gallon of water. Likewise, the devotees with consciousness level one, will not receive all the benefits of my lectures. But if you are in consciousness level seven or eight or nine, then you will draw a whole lot of benefits.

"For example, my daughter was a princess in her previous birth. I came to visit her father, a king in United Kingdom, as a saint. We met at the Westminster Abbey where I gave a speech about Eastern philosophy. Later the King invited me to dine with him in his palace. The king asked his daughter, the princess sitting here among you, to help me navigate her palace. I imparted some valuable life lessons to her, and she became highly impressed by the saint and hence became my daughter in this birth to learn more about life and consciousness. She will learn everything in this birth and be born a saint-cum-Neurosurgeon on consciousness level ten, the ultimate of consciousness, and she will teach humanity and be the grandest of teachers that the twenty-second century will ever see."

The crowd looked for SriSham's daughter, Rashmi. She was not there. She generally played upstairs with the children, telling SriSham she had homework to complete.

"Coming back to my co-passenger, he asked me about this saint." He pointed to the photo on the wall again. "I had not tried to strike up a conversation with him before that. I told him about the miracles of Maximovitch and Mother Drexel's miracles. She was recognized as a saint only in 2000. When New Mexico mentions the unassuming saint Tekakwitha, when apparitions are celebrated as miracles in your faith, you will all accept them. Then why not our saint? Think for a second."

No one in the crowd had heard of them. SriSham's biggest assets were his voracious reading habit and his ability to retain what he read. Every little detail of what he read resided in his brain or on the volumes of papers he brought with him on which he meticulously wrote down every detail. He reproduced them like there was no tomorrow, and they believed him. Nothing that he ever said was deemed a tall tale though they agreed that some of his stories could have been an innocent form of exaggeration. They did not have the time or patience to verify the names he mentioned in his orations. When they did, they discovered that history had something about every one of them.

"The co-passenger suddenly told me that he had visited all the Hindu temples in Houston and that no one had ever explained it so beautifully. He was convinced of our concepts of reincarnation and understood our celestial astral world and beings. I explained to him about syzygy. He was astounded. If anyone here knows what syzygy is?" SriSham did not give the crowd his answer. "As the topic is so elusive, you should elect to rationalize the understanding about these only in private since it would take many hours or even days to explain them."

SriSham loved private sessions as if he were a psychiatrist dispelling their doubts. He liked to throw in hard and seemingly high-sounding words. They did not stop to question him because of his command not to interrupt him during his dialogues since he would lose his train of thought. But they could write down their questions with their email address and give them to him after the discourse, and he would send them emails with his replies, he said.

SriSham continued. "When I compared the miracles of Jesus Christ to the miracles of our saint, he was spellbound. I gave him my email and assured him I would reply. After all, our saint is the one answering all my sixteen thousand or sixteen thousand and forty to be exact, emails a month."

No one interrupted to say, "We've never seen a Caucasian or an

African in our temples." But no one doubted that he was receiving over five hundred emails a day with questions.

SriSham kept at it. "And then he gave me his card, and I gave him our master's picture with my name on the back. He asked me if I was the saint, and I said, 'Yes, and I'm taking his message to the world. It's sans religion, and I am taking him on a golden platter to the world. So, I am he and he is me. At least that's how I feel.'"

SriSham waited for a few seconds to see if there was any opposition to his daring statement. Those who were not half-asleep had stomachs that were growling due to the aromas coming from the kitchen. These prayer sessions included elaborate dinners with several varieties of desserts at the end, and some devotees took home food enough for several days.

SriSham continued. "Our saint was very happy in the empty seat in another plane when Dr. Sheela, one of my Houston devotees, was traveling to Orlando from Houston. I was signaling to her happily about her practice."

He could not let go of a topic the boy on the stairwell was mocking him about, and no one knew who Dr. Sheela was. He felt it was important to authenticate his stories with names and designations; he said that most of his devotees were brilliant doctors and especially surgeons.

But SriSham would not give them any time to think. His practice was to continue with another story immediately. "Once, a devotee who owned a small grocery shop in Pearland was just feeling desolate and dragging himself through the aisles straightening things at the end of the day when things started levitating and magically moving around on their own and placing themselves on the shelves. I will give you just a taste of the incomparable one's miracles because not many of you will understand his miracles. In this day of science and technology, when your sons and daughters are ready to go to Yale, or Harvard, or Georgia Tech, who will believe what I am saying?"

He was fluent, glib, voluble.

"One day in Atlanta, a great devotee asked me if our saint was capable of only such fizzy, sparkling, cheap miracles. When my books come out, you will understand that when you come to this mentor, he will be capable of achieving the monumental, the extraordinary, feats such as dissolving your cancer cells and brain tumors and the simpler ones such as relieving you of your daily stress and tiredness. Your sons and daughters will get assistantships to work in Manhattan, the most expensive city in the world, and these are providential, promising, felicitous miracles. I ask him to fulfill every single whim and fancy of every one of my devotees".

SriSham was in love with many English words. 'Felicitous' was just one of them.

"He watches the political scenario closely. The recent laws in this country mandated that some Indian families pack their bags and go back to India," he said in spite of the fact that no such laws existed.

"'Stop packing!' I insisted." SriSham shouted the phrase "STOP" and he closed his eyes and continued in a softer voice that was hard to hear without paying full attention. "Our saint was indicating to me that they would *not* be leaving the country. Such are his miracles. He is capable of the jazzy as well as the graceful."

At that point, SriSham couldn't control his enthusiasm. "If you lose one job, our saint will give you two or three jobs." He pointed to a corner of the room. "That man lost a job for which he was being paid sixty thousand but got another one that paid him eighty thousand, and more offers are on the way. Ask Raj if that's not true."

Everyone turned in the direction he was pointing and tried to discern to whom he was pointing.

SriSham was a regular *Wall Street Journal* follower and read books on mergers and acquisitions. He wanted to say something that his educated listeners would believe. He hoped Dr. Kumar, his ex-wife's surgeon brother in Orlando, was listening. SriSham very dutifully read the *Harvard Business Review* for information he could use in his dialogues. "I know all the companies that will merge in the future. I know what stocks are going to blow through the roof and which will hit rock bottom. I can advise you what penny stocks to buy and how to manage the Bitcoin market if you are into that sort of thing. But I am not getting into that now since there's no time. If you say, 'No, Sri, I don't understand the Crypto-currency market,' I will say, 'Come to me or to our saint. We are one and the same. I, the mystic, will demystify the Bitcoin industry making it easier for you to understand anything under the sun or out of this world.'"

SriSham had advised his devotees to use the Sanskrit word *sri* to address him since there was no equivalent word that could convey the same or nearly a similar meaning in any other language. That three-letter word encompassed seventy-eight meanings; no word in the *Oxford English Dictionary* had so many interpretations, he confirmed with confidence.

"Every morning, he (points to the photograph on the wall) converses with me for forty-five minutes and up to three and quarter hours."

Forty-five minutes suddenly seemed insignificant to him, so he quickly added the hours to it as if to authenticate the conversations.

"He briefs me on some devotees' birthdays, anniversaries, or impending surgeries, and I call them the next day to wish them well, and they ask me 'How did you know this, Sri?' He notifies me of everything in advance. You will know all this too once you start repeating his one hundred and eight different names after me. Your dependence on him should be complete to the point that no one can question your devotion, not even yourself. Get to know him or at least get to know me. People who have been attending these prayer sessions are getting sudden and surprising results. It's like your Tesla going from zero to sixty in just a few seconds—they experience a sudden surge of good things happening in their lives."

SriSham wanted to add an indemnification clause, so he hurriedly added his usual doctrine of karma.

"But sometimes, the karmic route may take you on a loop. You may take I-315 and then you go to route 270 or 670. In this great travel, our saint may make you go around, but it's all your karma. Once you get rid of it by attending my discussions, you will travel on known paths. To get rid of your bad karma, I invite you to also recite his names one hundred and eight times just once a month, which will take about thirty minutes. The sponsors have timed it. You will receive unbelievable benefits. I will explain how to call his names. You will get sudden results."

SriSham noticed a devotee nearby giving off a big yawn and heard his stomach growling, so he said, "Listen carefully. Be here, now". SriSham had heard that advice through the internet given by a famous cousin of SriSham where she had given an interview to one of the newspapers of her town. That cousin of SriSham had come to be considered as an intelligent soul in their family. SriSham was impressed and it sat well with him as his past was not anything he wanted to remember. "Be here, now" he pronounced loudly. "Forget all of your past deeds, and do not worry about your future", he expanded on the idea. Later when he asked his devotees as to what they liked the most among his advices, one successful woman in the group said "Be here, now" was the best one ever. Ever since, SriSham started to follow that cousin everywhere. He went into her

FB stealthily on an everyday basis, watched her on the net constantly and repeated her words, in his lectures. They confirmed him they adhered to that one advice and felt good about their lives.

"After all, these are just thirty-minute lectures. Listen with absolute silence and devotion. I come to you only five times a month, four at the Children's class and one on this second Saturday, but I have interesting stories that are all true. I have told the story of the Seattle devotee who was in a bad plane accident and how he walked out of it without a scratch. He had a picture of our saint in his private jet. I can tell you the miracles of your great-great-grandchildren's whereabouts and their futures. I have interesting stories about everyone. They are all living in this country or India. I can tell you the story of the lady in Accra, the capital city of Ghana whose phone starts to chant on its own when she thinks of our saint. Get to know him fully well, or at least try to get to know me fully well so you will get answers. His performances are exalted ones, and since you are his devotees, your performance will not be any less."

An unusually big bug came in through the open doors since so much food sat on the dining table. SriSham called it the saint himself who had come out of the photograph to taste the food before giving it to his devotees. No one dared to cover the dishes or swat the bug or help it fly away after that pronouncement. The bug buzzed around every dish and finally chose one dessert and went inside. SriSham called it the favorite dish of their saint; he told them they were the luckiest group in all of Houston to have been visited by their saint and to be able to partake of a meal with him.

"I will give you a suitable example that all of you can verify. The 2017 Rose Bowl Championship game was going on, and it was a Monday. My senior officers at work said that number-five Penn State was playing number-nine USC. Who was the latter?" SriSham waited to see if anyone answered.

The boy on the stairwell said, "Trojans."

"Yes, the Trojans," SriSham said. "I do not know anything about football. Nobody likes football in my group of devotees either."

He arbitrarily brought them all under the roof of football haters. Since many of them were women, his comment went by haplessly.

"Anyway, I was at work, and my colleagues said, 'Okay, SriSham, you say you can predict 500 years into future, so tell us the results of this game.' I told them that USC would win, and they laughed at me. They said that Penn State was on a nine-game winning streak including a pivotal victory over number-two Ohio State. 'How could USC win?' they asked me. And USC won. When you are within our saint as I am, you will be able to see the future. I know the future of everybody including all CEOs, COOs, and CTOs, or if you are an artist or working for Wipro or Infosys. He shows me the future of each and every one of you, and I even know the current salaries of each and every one of you and your future salaries.

"The Boston devotee's salary came down from eighty-nine

thousand to forty thousand. I thought he would stop calling me, but then he called me." SriSham chuckled. "This is a scientific effect, I told this devotee. I asked this devotee to do this forty-K job for three months to get rid of all twenty-nine of his karmic years and then he would get a whopping one-hundred-K job and go to Rome for his own Roman Holiday, the 1953 movie with Gregory Peck and Audrey Hepburn."

The gathering gave out a feeble laugh here.

"He went to Rome because that was where his wife wanted to go. This had been predicted by me about a year before he went to Rome. Then this Boston devotee came back just to collect his huge bonus. This was Raman's effect. This one in the picture is the Lord Rama himself, and he causes all these great things for you. Never fear when you are in his presence."

SriSham alluded to the scientist Raman and his discovery which came to be called 'Raman's effect' to the Hindu God with the same name. He constantly brought science in his speeches imagining that he was captivating the younger generation. SriSham's speeches were disjointed, but they made it clear that his devotees were incapable of receiving their saint's grace without SriSham.

"I have been sent here to mold your characters, but you have been surrounded by a company with giant-sized egos. I will be on the periphery or perimeter."

SriSham was in love with that and many other words.

"Great free falls are mandatory and inevitable in all your lives, but I will stay here to catch you. Another devotee had had the world by the tail. She was making a killing at the drop of a dime as though she had a license to print money. Some of you know Mrs. Nooyi who achieves this. But this is not her. This one is a different 'She' devotee. She had the Midas touch, but everything suddenly came tumbling down for her. I told her not to cry over spilled milk. I consoled her and showed her ways to get back on the ride, and she started stealing the show again. After all, she's a PhD in molecular science. I told her she would own a blood bank and a human tissue plant in South Texas that would be worth millions. She dropped the phone from her hand in awe but bludgeoned me; she asked, 'Guruji, are you all right? What meds are you takin'?' I told her just as President Clinton once said, 'When I was in England, I experimented with marijuana a time or two, but I didn't like it, and I didn't inhale.' I was just joking. I'm sure you'll get it. The man in this photo is just too cool for us to understand him fully.

"I see the future. I have a compulsion to be in touch with either our saint or myself for your children's welfare. A Bangalore couple wanted their son to be married. They called me, and I contacted our saint in this photo, and he told me that the boy would be married within two months, by November, and he produced addresses of girls by opening his palms, and he gave them to me. There were nine girls. Some of the addresses had attached photographs. This young man was shy when it came to meeting girls, but I insisted that he met all of them, one by one. Our saint could have produced just one photo and said, 'This one will be his wife,' but our saint is generous; he gives us great choices."

Seeing the frown on one of the regular sponsor's daughter's face, SriSham quickly added, "This does not mean nine girls' contact information materialized from nowhere. It was a symbolic way of saying that this young man would eventually meet nine girls one after the other. I told his parents I would help them select the best. They kept saying it was very difficult for boys to find girls anymore in India. Why is that? The educated will show female infanticide as the reason but I would confidently say that it's because boys in India and their families have forgotten this saint. Of course, girls these days are very well educated and have every right to reject an alliance. Girls have every right to wait for men who make more money than they do.

"Another devotee wanted a nice boy for her granddaughter. She told me of her worries, and I resolved them. This saint will buy you homes in Chicago and New Delhi and provide you with good health, cars, and marriages. You will get so many benefits from attending this session every second Saturday.

"In so many churches around the world are paintings and icons that have wept on and off as a warning of dark days to come. Haven't you heard of Archangel Michael from Greece? They trumpet tearing-up statues of Jesus, the Virgin Mary, angels, and saints. Crying icons aren't unusual in churches. Some of the cases have been debunked as practical jokes or outright frauds and hoaxes, but in temples around the world, the statues of our saint are alive. Whenever I enter a temple that has a statue of our saint, he rises from his throne and comes to the door to welcome me. In temples where board members fought and squabbled over the presidency and power, the statue of our saint silently cried. Unable to bear the fights, he one day became alive, first took the form of a snake and chased them around the temple because I had earlier asked him not to come in his original form since that might shock the members and some of them may die from a sudden heart-attack. They attacked the snake with stones. Hence our Saint became too angry and then took his original form by shedding off his snake skin, appeared before them all naked (taking a side look at Emma when he said 'naked') and started shooting the same stones at them from his hand."

SriSham pointed his hand at some devotees as if it were a pistol and gave off sounds of gunshots.

"The temple board members were all shocked beyond belief. He could not stand the political problems and gave them a jolt to resolve it immediately. A few days before this extreme, I tried to warn the members saying that the statue in their temple was crying, but they had brushed me aside. Once they got over their shock, they called me and apologized.

"Goes to prove that if you pay attention to me and my teachings, your sons and daughters will become valedictorians. My Freemont devotee's son got an eighty-nine in mathematics but wanted a ninety, so he called me. I said, 'So be it,' and he never got less than a ninety after his call to me."

The stairwell boy mumbled something about why the boy had not asked for a ninety-five or ninety-nine instead of a ninety when he could have received that as easily. His mother glared at him, and he quieted down.

"You have to respect the person who reveals your future without erring. How many of you know I carry on continuous conversations with this man in the picture every night for three hours? I can see through your bodies. How else could I have told Mrs. Rojas that her husband's heart valve was clogged? I asked them to see the surgeon right away. I do not know how doctors fix this. Any cardiologists here?"

SriSham stopped and observed the crowd, which fell into hushed silence looking for a cardiologist. Having doctors in his discourses was extremely important for him. He hoped that his first wife's surgeon brother in Florida was watching his live performance that Emma was videoing.

"They went to the doctor the next day, and the surgeon told them of the urgency of the situation and operated on him. He's doing fine now. You are now thinking, 'Can he see through our bodies?' My answer is a resounding yes."

Emma smiled at him, and he smiled freely back at her.

"You can test me on this. Yesterday, a devotee who had come home the day before from the hospital asked me, 'Please tell me which part of my body was operated on.' Without waiting even for a fraction of a second or batting an eye, I said his head. Later, it was confirmed that he had Parkinson's disease. Where else would they put the nodes on but his brain, right? Call it ESP, or sixth sense, or precognition. This is not clairvoyance, but it is much better than prediction." He did not admit that Parkinson's showed a lot of outward symptoms.

Most in the crowd understood the word *prediction* but not the word *clairvoyance*.

"This is a spiritual blessing given only to some in this world. Such things can be yours when you attend my one-hour name-calling sessions regularly."

The boy on the stairwell laughed audibly.

SriSham said that he had catapulted into somewhat of a higher inclusion and therefore into the inversions of the saintly world. He said he would lecture separately on inversion, the condition of being turned inward, and that those interested could approach him to be included in those classes.

Those of the first generation born in the United States were made to attend SriSham's session by their parents. Children ages three to fifteen played upstairs since they would create such commotion during the sessions that SriSham was continually shushing them. The older children were not allowed to be upstairs; they did not have much of a choice but to listen to SriSham. SriSham's English was good, so they understood what he was saying, but their mistrust was obvious. Some eighteen-year-old said SriSham's claims were outrageous dubbing them into one category 'bluff'. They saw right through his harmless bragging as some of them called it, but their millionaire elders considered him the humble saint himself who had come back to them because of their good deeds. They became his ardent devotees since all his claims were absolutely true and they felt his presence when challenging life-situations resolved easily. The connection happened for them, they said, while they considered the kids as too young to attain that connection. No one identified him as a constant liar.

SriSham said he had gone to the smallest towns and the largest cities to make the Indian communities there better. There would be no more sitting on the sidelines. Their saint, and therefore he himself, encompassed all the gods of all the religions of the world. SriSham claimed that he had communicated with half a million or more people. He was a mystic; he could stay in Houston and be present in New Delhi simultaneously. He named all the devotees who saw him in New Delhi when he had actually been in Texas working, but no one demanded any authentication for any of his claims, not that any of them were interested in such substantiation.

"One Houston devotee who is right here today asked me to conduct this prayer session, which we are about to embark on for eleven days in their beautiful, multimillion-dollar home, and then very good results came. His son started studying well, and other problems were resolved. It's late in Washington, DC. It's ten p.m. But today is what?" When no one answered him, he said, "Today is—Saturday!" SriSham said it as if it were a revelation. "So, it's okay if I went over five minutes."

That lecture had been unusually long. SriSham did not realize that he had spoken for well over ninety minutes. The fact that they were there for him for two hours was proof- enough for him. A reassurance that they still accepted him as their saint's deputy or saint himself after his absence of two months and the passing away of his second wife during a holy trip was indispensable for him.

"Again, when this San Jose devotee—sorry, but I cannot name this devotee because his case became very famous, but you can google this—was languishing in jail framed by police because of his skin color, his wife called me and said that there were twenty-five formidable witnesses to testify against her husband. I said, 'Don't worry. I will come as your only witness to court since they are overlooking a major point of contention.'

"I asked her to send a picture of our saint or me to the penitentiary. The accused himself called me, and I told him that I would take the stand for him and he would be acquitted on the third Monday of the following month. The witnesses who took the stand were very incoherent. The state's attorney failed to meet the burden of proof on all charges. The California district attorney had not coached them well. The judge banged his gavel and said, 'You are a free man.'

"And one time, I went to a store in Sugarland near the Meenakshi Temple. I gave a photo of our saint to the store manager and told her that her husband would be released from jail. She was stunned. I had never seen them before".

"I now notice that this new house has cameras and a good security system. I told Soori, our host not to engage it. The picture of our saint on the wall is a fantastic postmodern security system in itself since our saint is watching every move of everyone here."

His devotees straightened themselves and looked at the picture again.

"The lavish home of Sunder Pi aka Sundhar Picchai, Google's CEO, does not have any security system, only our saint's picture. I know that because I have been there." SriSham was getting bolder. "It is also true that one of our former Prime Ministers, whom I am not mentioning by name due to security reasons, do not have security systems in their home, but just our Saint's' huge photograph on the foyer"

"There are a lot of great gurus coming from India to Houston promising good futures right and left, but nothing is happening. They are all meeting with me this week. Let me not meander. There are so many great swamis, but none can see through your body as I can. I am the one who can do that as far as I know. The paraplegic child, who took a strong leukemia treatment, Uhmmmm, I have not told you the story of the paraplegic child. What was her name?".

He looked at Emma, who said, "Krishna."

"Yes, the two-year-old, Krishna in St. Louis. She was cured completely when I entered her home. She came running to me and fell in prostration at my feet." SriSham pointed to his feet with all his fingers. "These become the feet of that incomparable one when you have trust and fall on them. If you have questions about your life, He will give me answers in my dream. When I introduce him to you, welcome him with a red flower. Perform this prayer—chant his names one hundred and eight times. That is the king of all prayers that will give you anything you want.

"Every bit of what I say is happening and has happened. I can also expound on the miracles of tomorrow. There's hardly anything that will happen to you that I do not know. I have access to all your lives. When somebody can see through your body and say your gallbladder will be infected and your mitral valve will be defective in five years, you listen well. This is not telekinesis. These are real stories. I can give you their phone numbers if you want including a ballet-dancer with a back problem. I have several pages of examples, but it's very late in Washington, DC, and hundreds of devotees are watching me in Rome and Switzerland. I will wrap up. Emma knew SriSham had used some of his favorites words in the last few sentences, 'paraplegic' and 'telekinesis'. Emma understood him like the back of her palm.

His examples of sicknesses were mostly cases of women. He said women were prone to get dangerous diseases than men. Men got hospitalized only when it was someone else's mistake – an accident that was caused by someone or by God to punish them for not attending his sessions. SriSham said he did not stay with the surgeons while they were operating on his female devotees to respect their modesty should they meet him after the surgery.

"This is a very powerful phenomenon in your lives. When I introduce you to him, he will change your life. I am very proud to introduce my great mentor to all of you. When I introduce you to him, I know he will resolve all your problems. You may say all of you know him already thus no introductions are needed, but without someone in whom our saint confides every night, it's impossible to reach him directly the way you ought to in order to receive all the benefits I have narrated to you already. Surely, he has established a rapport with me, but it is not possible for him to establish the same rapport with every one of you. You have to be in the ninth dimension of your lives to be able to know Him fully let alone to negotiate with him. Don't ask me what the ninth dimension is. It would take me a month to explain it. If you privately want to contact me about it, please do."

SriSham wrapped up his discourse by thanking the gathering and saying that he might not be up to meeting people privately to hear their problems and give directions that day since he felt indisposed due to his travels. He told them, however, that if their inquiries were urgent, he would meet with them individually. He said that he wanted to go home after the chanting; his devotees could email their questions to him.

"Now let's start the most sensible chanting on this planet that will be chanted on Mars, Jupiter, Mercury, and the moon pretty soon. The wives here should know that in some congregations, women are not allowed to chant this prayer or say even one name of our saint because women cannot bear the ferocity of the chanting. Do you all remember the incident in Charlotte? Mothers and daughters came to recite and were sent back by the priest. But I will let everyone recite. It is perhaps more important that women be in tune. Get ready, please."

The boy on the stairwell came up front since he was the only son of the parents sponsoring the event that evening. SriSham asked for more water. The boy's mother asked him to fetch a cup of water, and he brought it in a Styrofoam cup; they were to be used by everyone except the master.

After the short chanting, the devotees came in line, fell onto SriSham's feet or bent down and touched his feet, and received random blooms of shriveling flowers in their outfits or in plastic bags. SriSham kept urging them to plant the filaments in a pot and a beautiful flowering tree would grow in their homes. Then they were to plant the trees in their yards and put up signs that read, "If you see a rare flowering tree in Houston, take it home."

"After all," he told them, "You can grow new ones from the blown sepals."

It required some thirty minutes for all to pass by SriSham. They all got close to him, collapsed at his feet, touched them, took a drop of the oil, and fell prostrate again before the picture of their saint adorned with garlands and drapery bound in graceful loops. He insisted that they take flowers from his hand only. Emma took photos of each family with SriSham, and then the devotees were allowed to enter the dining room where a grand spread awaited them.

It had taken about two and a half hours before they were in the dining room—an hour and thirty minutes for SriSham's discourse, thirty minutes for chanting, and then thirty minutes in line to throw themselves at SriSham's feet, receive the banged-up flowers, and pose for photographs. Some were pleased that SriSham fostered their cultural traditions; they stood by him for photos that SriSham said would be published in his upcoming book. They considered it treacherous to pass up the opportunity to be photographed with the myriad-minded mystic. He asked his younger crowd to read his books instead of *Harry Potter* because it was magic that the author dealt with in those books and that nothing happened with magic unless it was due to his saint.

He related a story of a man who had been in a coma. SriSham had gone to this man's room in the ICU, made him sit up as though from a deep sleep, and made him eat a big breakfast. It was as though he could not risk leaving any scenario untouched.

Emma wandered around with camera in hand. As people stood in line, SriSham often left his spot and moved brushing Emma from behind to meet and greet devotees who were not in the line. He took his own sweet time to come back to his spot for his feet to be touched and to offer the bow that would grow into a flowering tree if only they attended SriSham's chanting sessions regularly. His secret and invisible hands were to be trusted absolutely for everything to happen as per the devotees' desires.

The feast in the dining room was lavish—*chaat*, *papri*, and *dhokla* were among the appetizers. Main courses included saffron *pulao*, *naan*, *matar panner*, *chapattis*, *chana masala*, potatoes and cauliflower *korma*, homemade yogurt, pickles, and *papad*. The desserts were *jamoons*, *kheer*, and *kulfi*, eggless cake for the elderly, carrot *halva*, and *mango lassi*, SriSham's favorite.

Many such dialogues had occurred in Houston over the past few years since SriSham had moved there from OSU (Ohio State University), Ohio. He narrated stories about a devotee's myopia being cured when SriSham applied the oil to his eyes, and the same thing had happened to people suffering from psoriasis or shingles. Autism was cured. Teachers and parents of children with special education needs called or emailed him saying 'they were special children once, not anymore but just normal children now'. People he cured called him God, SriSham said.

Someone's eyes that had nine holes in them had been cured. He had asked someone whose blood pressure was 180/80 to stop taking Lisinopril and Metoprolol. He asked them if they were HIV positive because he could ask such questions while doctors could not. He called these people his cases as if he were a doctor, and he would tell those in Washington that those he cured were in San Jose; he told those in San Jose that those he cured were elsewhere as well.

SriSham knew one family from Boston who had once invited him to perform the rituals at their home; he addressed them as Boston Brahmins connoting great wealth, political influence, and far-reaching philanthropic works. The family lived in a townhome near Harvard Square. SriSham said he had been invited to speak in Harvard but he had declined due to lack of time. He said that generations of scholars and CEOs had been inviting him to their homes, but no one recognized their names.

SriSham had developed sleepwalking symptoms; he would get up at three, walk to the kitchen of his apartment, and hear exactly the same steps from the apartment above him. He tested the theory by making other noises such as opening the fridge or crunching cereal, and he heard those noises as well coming from above him. This story about himself changed; he said that a devotee had complained of noises from above. When SriSham confronted the devotee's upstairs neighbor about the matter, he said, he bought her a house, so she could move out thus resolving the problem for his devotee. No one asked why he hadn't just bought a house for his devotee.

When devotees showed up late to his meetings, he insisted that his saint, who was alive in the picture, became distressed since it kept them from knowing him. SriSham's advice was that they essentially start some thirty minutes earlier.

He said his saint could flick a matchstick—he demonstrated this by igniting an imaginary match—and set fire to their goals and throw stones at them. He said he would have to try to appease his saint and plead on behalf of the latecomers by giving him many red roses. SriSham put three red roses, one for each family that had walked in late one time, under the picture of the saint.

He would credit the success of his ten-dollar millionaires to the generosity of the saint; he would say, "I was there always with them. There could be no other reason for their success."

For most of them, it had been a methodical process—reach the United States, stay with a relative for a few months until finding a job and a small apartment that was shared with other Indian immigrants, and travel in a shared vehicle. After a few years, go back to India to find a very well-educated techno girl, both work for a few years, invest one salary carefully, and not spend without reason. They ran like horses with blinders on, looking only straight ahead just working and investing. The mantra was - work, invest; work, invest; work, invest. By age forty, they had made it.

Many of them came to this country to do a PHD. That gave them the golden ticket to enter this country. It also gave them the leeway to stay here for several years as their dissertations got rejected a few times. After a PHD they had a regular job with a decent pay and a teaching gig at night. They were contributors.

The new and young Y2K crowd was different. There were many of them. They had good company. They brought their own live entertainment from India. They saw no need to mingle with anyone other than their own clan. These were worker bees. The early settlers who came in the 70s and 80s came on their own nudge. There were not many of them. They were good in the written word since they learned English from the horse's mouth. What was common with both groups was that none wanted to leave America.

SriSham asked his tech team to improve his access to his devotees. "They can now see me and the Prayer-session. I should be able to see them," he insisted. "In our next discourse, I want to see Prime Minister Modi, Google CEO Sunder Pi, and Obama, whom I am expecting to join us soon."

However outrageous his claims were, Houstonites invited him maybe because he came cheap. A temple priest invited for a ceremony at a home cost at least two hundred dollars for him and another two hundred dollars as a gift to temple. Some of them were pitifully inadequate in their language skills that were rueful, and everything got lost in the translation of Sanskrit *shlokas*. SriSham's English was impeccable; he used no high-sounding Sanskrit words, and he charged nothing. He would give to the children the little they collected for him when they answered his questions.

His perspicacious self, instead of immerged in the dossier at the table, sometimes, led himself to act in a frenetic, *katzenjammer* manner and created disorder among his gullible devotees. Emma kept his tchotchkes about him during his frenzies. SriSham was a teetotaler and non-smoker. That was enough for the crowd. The crowd said that his frenzies happened since he saw their Saint then.

SriSham requested his devotes to cover his books (once they came out) in yellow (for ladies only) and in gray (for guys only) and keep them as scriptures, their constant companions. That would make everything happen for them as per their wishes. If they ever saw his books move by themselves, they were not to be alarmed—that meant SriSham or his saint had gone in there to reside or resolve a question or problem for them. Emma confirmed that they were to be published the following summer.

SriSham was the hero of all his stories; he was always the winner;

if facts got in the way, he distorted or ignored them; facts also morphed into whatever he wanted them to be; His exaggerations verged on falsehoods. He was in love with the United States—its language, attitude, and unending products, and his ability to own and enjoy them.

He was either a bully, a villain who sought utter control, or a pitiable, sick man who was desperate for compassion, mercy, and love.

CHAPTER 3

SriSham had grown up in Vellore, in southern India, a city in the state of Tamil Nadu. His household had absolutely no appreciation for trees or plants. His father had high standards for his two boys. SriSham's brother was four years his younger.

SriSham's father, a man of few words, insisted that he attend Harvard, Oxford, or Cambridge. He taught him flawless English, mathematics, and the local language. He expected him to stand first in every subject at school; he would not hear of SriSham's obtaining anything less than 95 percent in any subject.

SriSham was a good student, but he was never good enough for his father. He completed an engineering degree in India and applied to many master's degree programs that his father was enamored of, but after learning he would not get into any of them, he applied to colleges of a lesser caliber in the United States.

His father's passing had necessitated SriSham's finding employment to support the family of three. Thoughts of studying in the United States took a back seat.

Marriage proposals started knocking on his door; he was a degreed man with a job. After he carefully looked at all the photographs, credentials, resumes, biodata of girls that this uncle or that aunt recommended, the 'hopefuls' were set aside. Then the process of elimination began. They zeroed in on Ambika.

SriSham was enamored of her; she was from New Delhi, a faraway, modern city compared to Vellore. In the photograph, she was wearing a ladies' version of a Nehru suit. Her high snood of hair brought her to his height. One white rose stuck out from behind an ear. He and his mother were shocked to see that she wore no jewelry. Almost every other photograph showed girls with chunky chokers and the archetypal temple-ware studded with gold coins and bangles that hid the girls' hands.

"Daughter of a rigid military officer?" asked SriSham's mother.

"Yes, mother. That's good for girls," SriSham said with a chuckle.

"Why is it good for girls?"

"Military lifestyle at home. Inflexible officers raise proper daughters. She would've had directives to come home before seven in the evening wherever she went," he said with a crooked smile as he stared at her photograph. He looked creepy even to his mother.

"But she doesn't know the local language here. How will she manage without being able to converse with vendors and peddlers?" She shuffled some photographs. "How about this girl from Kerala, our neighboring state?" The Keralite had strung vintage gold bullets on a necklace to advertise her riches.

The kind mother had projects to complete before her household would welcome a bride. The attic was open; she desired doors to be installed. She considered their dreary, wet bathroom and commode unsuitable for the derriere of a young woman. The entire house cried for new paint.

"Mother, don't you know they practice black magic in Kerala? Not to mention they're ultra-leftists?"

Kerala had been the first state in India to achieve a hundred percent literacy, and it had the nation's largest politically aware population. It housed the biggest Communist party in India that was led by the Left Democratic Front. There also was the Indian National Congress led by the United Democratic Front since the late 1970s. Kerala had achieved a level of education that no other state in India had, but at the same time, the rumors of its sorcerers were also popular. This was like the two sides of a coin, on the one hand, a lot of people were well educated and on the flip of that coin, its villagers were rumored to have been practicing black magic bringing-in a lot wealth to Kerala.

"Shyam, I don't know anything about left or right, but don't believe that sorcery stuff. The educated do not. Just don't generalize reading something from a seditious, third-grade newspaper. The Keralite girl holds an engineering degree as you do, and they are all very well-placed people jobwise in their household."

His mother had the correct pronunciation of his name. Every time she addressed him, she included the *y* for the softness it brought, a sweet tapioca marmalade that melted on the tongue. SriSham liked the way she addressed him.

"Ma, I don't want an engineer, I want a wife. This girl from the north is only a BA, and that's in economics. If I wanted a BE, a professional, I would have gone for Parvathi, my old classmate, who was all over me." A chuckle came out of SriSham.

"Parvathi's family was loaded, Shyam. Parvathi's household had three cars. They would debate whether to take the red or white car for grocery shopping. That's not us. I heard she is in the US now."

SriSham showed his irritation. "Mother, can we deliberate about the proposal we have in our hands? I'm a man of exactitude by nature."

"This girl, Ambika, seems to hold a good position in the local army base. Will she leave her job and come all the way here?"

Southern India was an island unto itself when it came to the wars India fought. The reminiscences were rare, war devastation was rarer, and soldiers but a comparatively few, so not many army bases were in the southern parts of India in the late eighties and early nineties.

"Mother, It's only a bookkeeping job. Her father must have pulled it for her in the barracks. Why not come down here to be an engineer's wife? Even one lakh rupees of dowry will not give her a husband like me."

"Army people do not believe in giving dowries to their daughters, and you always said you knew many girls who would simply give you a lakh without questioning."

"That military officer is not required to give me anything if he doesn't want to. Now don't be asking them for a dowry and this and that."

It was now her turn to laugh. "Shyam, I never wanted anything. You were the one to gloat and gyrate constantly about your worth in the marriage market. I was just thinking of some repairs to the house before the bride steps in. Now don't you worry. I won't open my mouth in front of your future in-laws. And they might want the marriage to take place in New Delhi. Their friends and relatives might be around that area."

"No way my wedding will happen in New Delhi—too far away for my friends to attend."

Obsessing over Ambika, SriSham went to New Delhi. He was apprehensive about meeting her small family, but he was eager to do so. He felt intimidated right from the start by the picture-perfect garden and servants in every corner as though lurking to pounce in protection and waiting for commands. He regretted not buying better shoes for the journey.

So much of love is physical attraction—at least in the beginning. Ambika stood above all the ubiquitous, serious southerners. Their marriage took place in New Delhi much to SriSham's dislike, but he was mesmerized by her and did not object. He gave a grand reception in a hotel for his friends and relatives back home.

Ambika did not want to quit working. Her job turned out to be a high-ranking government position, and she insisted that SriSham get a transfer up north. His company had no branch in New Delhi, so they settled for what was then called Bombay. SriSham's reluctance to move there sowed the first seed of discord in his wedded bliss; Ambika was oblivious to his obvious frustration at that.

He had no knowledge of the local languages, Hindi and Marathi, while Ambika was fluent in Hindi with her Delhi upbringing, and she eased into office work and shopping.

SriSham was beset by cynicism, a new job he had not gotten used to, his laziness that compounded the problems he faced at work, a crowded new city and new language, a mind full of negativity, all-encompassing aggression, and a jaded prey.

They had their first son just before their first anniversary. She had wanted to go to her parents' place in Delhi to deliver the baby; that was customary as expectant mothers thought that was how they would receive the best postpartum care. For SriSham, there was nothing to think about. Delhi was cooler and much less rainy than Bombay was.

SriSham's mother went from Vellore to Bombay to cook and care for her son now that he was going to live a bachelor's life until Ambika came back from Delhi with their firstborn. But two or three months later, there still had been no sign of Ambika's return. He became unable to bear his mother's insistent pleas for him to go to Delhi or at least write to Ambika.

SriSham was an angry young man who had not hesitated to beat his wife up if things did not go his way. Ambika made it clear that she was not coming back. She didn't want SriSham to see the newborn either.

"Shyam, get me a ticket to Delhi. I want to take their pulse myself. I want to see them and bring them back."

Her appeals turned to begging, so SriSham got her a plane ticket to New Delhi.

Much to her disappointment, a household servant of Ambika's showed up at the airport and drove her to Ambika's parents' abode. Ambika's father was at work, and Ambika's family's lukewarm reception of her was explained after tea and toast.

"Do you know that your son tortured my daughter all the ten months they were married? What should have been a honeymoon period for a young woman was nothing less than hell."

The forlorn mother had come expecting misery but not of that magnitude.

"I missed all the signs in the very first months during my visits to my daughter in Bombay. I noticed her weight loss. That should've been my cue. I should have realized it right then and there."

Ambika's mother blamed herself. In India, a newly married girl losing weight was a bad sign. That meant the girl was not being fed properly or had to work too hard or both.

Ambika came out of her room and narrated everything that SriSham had done to her. He had beaten her, used a poor choice of words while conversing with her, suspected her constantly about her work and salary, and mocked the way she moved her hips when SriSham's brother had come to stay with them for two days while she served him lunch.

"Your son was on me every single night. Even on days I was totally spooked, he was creepy, indulged, relentless ..." She stopped for a minute watching SriSham's mother's expression; she seemed to be crying, but Ambika was not going to speak in euphemisms. "Oh, I know what you would say—just lie there. That's what your generation of womenfolk would say. In fact, that is what my own mother would say if not explicitly. Was your son's father like him? Did he beat you up every day? Surely this lambasting has been fashioned on someone."

Ambika's mother chimed in. "Obviously, yours must have been a dysfunctional family."

"Do you know what the last straw was that broke this camel's back?" Ambika gesticulated with hands in the air as if to emphasize her question. "He asked me to abort this child when we came to know about my pregnancy. The reason was that ..."—she searched for the best words— "that ... that ... that all my family members, including my mother, had daughters the first time. Your wonderful son wanted only a son!" She laughed hysterically.

Sorrow destroyed their faces; the three women were engulfed by an uneasy silence, a strange unifying factor. The Vedas put it this way: "Every place where women are treated with respect, there God Himself dwells." The all-pervasive, grand, poet master Bharathi, who was akin to none other than Shakespeare, said, "To be born a woman, one had to have accomplished great penance in many previous births."

A mere mortal had annihilated the overwrought hearts of a new grandmother who had come to plead with her daughter-in-law to come back to her son, an educated, sensible, young new mother, and another woman with a wondrous man in tow, a pillar of support, for a husband. A strange company was united on a point not so coherently understood by any of them but a mantra their society repeated so often if not in so many words.

Ambika started crying quietly in the corner chaise hugging her newborn. "I was a dunce to marry him. I was too humiliated to discuss his cruelty with my parents."

Ambika's mother drew close to her daughter. "Abbi, please don't cry. I cannot bear this. It's also not good for a new mother, you have been depressed quite a bit, and you're nursing the little fellow. Please go on to your room and rest. I'll put on the record player."

Ambika got up to leave. She told SriSham's mother, "Tell him he did get a son, but he will grow up to be *my* son, who will never see that hammerhead, lunatic. I will never go back to him. I don't want him to even see my son's face. I want to bring my son up in the company of good fellows. Not all men are bad, you know, not *all* men." Such reassuring reiteration gave her some consolation. "This world is full of brothers who are so much better than the likes of your son. Tell your son I would bring up this boy to grow up to be a gentleman like my father and my brother."

Ambika's father arrived in the evening and welcomed SriSham's mother warmly. He asked if Chaarumathi, his wife, had given her the special Darjeeling tea that wasn't available down south. Not waiting for her answer, the gentleman took a peek inside his kitchen.

"Chaaru, did you get the Marsala tea for Amma?"

He addressed me as Amma! SriSham's mother thought. She was moved and did not feel alienated anymore. Such a heartening gesture. That was magic for a soul longing for compassion and rest. An easy fix—a kind, gentle word. That's all that was necessary but missing, and that's what she had lacked her entire life. In southern India, anytime one wanted to show he or she had a loving heart did so by using that word. It showed endearment, respect, love, heart, and gratitude all in a mushy, gooey, mind-melting awesomeness bound to make the one who was called Amma completely surrender. This word used to address a mother can be used to denote anyone whom one loves and respects abundantly. Dad to daughter, sister to sister, lover to sweetheart, brother to sister, a chauffeur, a boss, a fellow employee, a lover, a beggar for a surefire way of getting alms—all who heard it realized they were being shown love, not patronization.

Ambika's father asked her to extend her stay for a couple of days and join them to witness the Republic Day Parade before leaving.

"Amma, have you seen the live parade any time before?" he asked.

"No, I haven't." She felt his sincerity and honesty.

"Then you must stay. We have the best front-row seats. You will enjoy this," he said.

She welcomed the invitation on many levels; it bought her more time to persuade Ambika as well as enjoy the much-warranted break and leisure that she had never known. SriSham's mother had come to live a paltry, misery existence on this planet with utmost happiness in her heart. She had lost her father when she was two as she had heard from her mother. She had lived with her mother and a maternal uncle until she got married to SriSham's father at the tender age of fourteen. She had come to live with him when she was sixteen and had her first child at eighteen. Though she was forty-nine, she could very easily count the number of outings she had had as well as the number of movies she had seen, that being the only entertainment of her era. She had spent her life taking care of SriSham's father, his parents, and her two boys. Her stay there and the outing was more than welcome—a time of diversion from her family's shenanigans.

The uniformed young troopers marching in preparation for the parade she saw out the window were stunning.

On the morning of the parade, Ambika's father was wearing his medals and ribbons on his jacket—full-sized medals of the tri-lions facing three sides, the national emblem with Asoka-chakra in the center. He tucked his army hat in between his arm and torso to drink a second cup of tea. He gave his shoes a final shine before leaving the house.

"Father, you look trim and handsome," Ambika beamed as he opened the door of their jeep and helped all the ladies in. He held the infant until Ambika got in and carefully handed him to her bending his six-foot self, down in the back seat.

As he closed the door behind the three women, he asked Ambika if she wanted to sit up front in the jeep with him. She let out a shrill "Yes, Dad!" and her mother took the infant from her.

The brisk ride to the parade that morning, the joyous wishes she got from everyone as they drove, and Ambika and her highly decorated officer of a father with integrity and in uniform singing patriotic songs in Hindi she knew positively mesmerized her.

After the short ride, they got off the jeep, and officers saluted him. Many hands were extended for the infant. The army husband helped his wife out of the jeep; her silk Banaras sari and high snood of hair appeared without a wrinkle. The party took turns congratulating Ambika on the new arrival. The breakfast spread that awaited them inside made her hungry. Their lifestyle was not anything as she had imagined.

This man, this wonderful man, and all the glory that he earned for himself with his hard work has rubbed off on his family, SriSham's mother thought. He automatically took care of the people around him. And Ambika, this new mother, had become a child herself riding in the front seat with her favorite dad. She wished her son was there to see this new Ambika with her father and mother.

The display of India's military prowess under Prime Minister Indira Gandhi, the weapons, the jets, the artillery and arsenal, the salutes—this was a world of its own. *Soldiers with automatic weapons hanging from their strong shoulders, paratroopers running to their posts without cringing—Ah, they are all carrying out their duties! They love their country and its people. They're willing to make the ultimate sacrifice, and it shows on their faces!* she thought. The everyday duties were practice, practice, practice from morning to evening. The aura was humbling. They radiated the nobility of their cause.

SriSham's mother felt that her son was the enemy of this father. *SriSham should be won over before he becomes this gentleman's nemesis!* she thought. He was the bulwark holding back floods from her son's life. Mistakes were made, but hopes do not have to be totally crushed.

Many men in uniforms thronged over to converse with Ambika and her mother after the parade. The military father had gone off with a group of buddies. Watching the uniformed and armed soldiers hug one another with greetings emphasized their optimism.

SriSham's mother could not discern Ambika's father's rank. Neither he nor his family had mentioned it. After constantly hearing engineers' and doctors' self-proclamations at home, his lack of ego was noble.

After lunch, they drove home. Ambika, her mother, and her father took such good care of the infant.

When SriSham's mother took leave of the family, Ambika had calmed down, and her father promised to help mend their relationship. A neatly packed parcel of Darjeeling pekoe tea and Kashmir apples accompanied her home. She considered Ambika's father's words to be gold. But she dreaded what her son would say when she got back without Ambika and his son, and she was right to dread that.

It didn't take two days for the mother to become brokenhearted again. She tried her best to talk sense to her son about going to New Delhi, apologizing, and bringing his wife and son back.

"Shyam, please come here and sit down," she said as she pointed to a dining table chair. Ambika had impeccable taste when it came to decorate their apartment. SriSham came in reluctantly but did not sit. His anger knew no bounds. He looked as if he wanted no connection to Ambika's world.

"Your father was an angry man, SriSham. He sent me to my mother's home for your delivery only the day before you were born, did you know? Everyone in my family was upset that I had arrived in a bus just one day before delivering you. When my mother asked your father about it when he came to see you, do you know what your father's reply was? 'No child will be born before the end of nine months.' He behaved like an idiot in front of my mother. He touched my waist in between my sari and blouse in front of my mother as though he were tickling me. My mother hated your father. She never came to visit me. She couldn't stand your father's arrogance. I kept quiet because I wanted a peaceful home for you and your brother."

The acknowledgement of his younger brother made SriSham resent his mother. "Okay, now!" His rude interruption shocked her. "Enough of this lecture. You've told me incredible stories about my father. Let's not go there!"

He pushed his feeble mother out of his way as he stormed out of the room, and she fell to the floor hitting her head on the wall. Shocked, SriSham ran to her and lifted her wailing, "Are you okay? Oh Mother, I'm so sorry. Me and my anger! Are you okay?"

SriSham's mother got up but was still in shock. "I'm okay, I'm okay." She just sat on the floor. SriSham picked her up and sat her in a chair. He apologized profusely and massaged her head, hands, and toes. He got her an aspirin.

Sitting on the chair calmly and looking around, she felt it strange that SriSham had many female goddesses on the altar. Bemused, she said, "There's no dearth of deities on pedestals in your apartment.

There's Saraswathi, goddess of knowledge, Lakshmi for wealth, and Durga, the embodiment of valor. Could Ambika be any different?"

"That wretched female, Ambika's mother, set them up here when she visited."

"Maybe she realized your disrespect for her daughter and was trying to tell you something. Shyam, prejudice is in blood. We hardly ever recognize it. I had the habit of pouring water over the washed dishes, washed by our maid. I could not take them in to my kitchen and put them away because the last person who touched them was the maid. I understood my prejudice only when someone pointed this habit out. Shyam, come here and sit with me. I want to tell you something. Do you do remember your uncle, your father's older brother, Varadhan?"

SriSham vividly remembered his physician uncle. SriSham and his brother had been constants at his new bungalow there in Madras, now Chennai. How could he forget? Weddings, baby showers, summer holidays, Marina Beach, road trips to Pondicherry, Sri Aurobindo Ashram, and Mahabalipuram with mammoth stone statues, chariots, and steps leading to the beach, all on the shores of the roaring Indian Ocean. *Wow! Those were the days!* he thought. SriSham and his younger brother yearned for their Madras trips as they called them.

Uncle Varadhan was the first one to own an automobile in their families. His children called it *"Papa's* Austin". It was a vintage 1950

Austin A40. They owned it until 1970 and sold it off to buy a brand-new 'Ambassador' which was manufactured in India. Dr. Varadhan took the boys and his children in his car graciously. Uncle Varadhan would drive them back to Vellore after their summer holidays.

"Your uncle Varadhan was a good man, but he had a loose tongue and a monstrous ego. Like our family, your father's sister's family would also be there for the holidays. Once when your aunt complained to Varadhan, her brother, about the bouts of dizziness she was having, he arrogantly ignored her illness and said she was just putting on an act for her relatives! She wept her heart out that night in the ladies' room because her brother had called her a liar in front of many people she respected. She cursed him to her heart's content. I shudder even now when I think of that night. In that spree, she didn't leave our family out. She cursed all children in her brother's family; she wanted them to be shattered as her heart had been shattered by Uncle Varadhan's words."

"Mother, how's this relevant?"

"I don't want her curses to affect anyone, Shyam."

"You're afraid I will suffer the same fate of Uncle Varadhan's sons?"

Dr. Varadhan's sons had been academically well bred but were as arrogant as their father. They were playboys who did not work; they lived off their physician father's investments. One had even been incarcerated for a long time. In those days, the rich never got arrested.

They bribed their way out. But Dr. Varadhan refused to bail his son out. His children lived a life of misery.

"Shyam, be cognizant of the lives of your elders. Do not take their paths if they are not delightful or enchanting. Be humble, learn to ask for forgiveness, and be a good man. Go apologize to Ambika's father. He will help you and your son. You must ask for his blessings and forgiveness by literally falling onto his feet." She finished instilling some fear into his aggravated self. *If my love did not do the work, the terror would, she thought.*

"Okay, mother," SriSham said in a subdued tone. "I'll go to Delhi. I promise to behave well in front of that idiot of a father" (using his mother's words, verbatim) "and bring Ambika back. Tell me, mother, is her father going to support her, all her life? Her brother is a good-for-nothing. Did you know he didn't pass his last board exams? Do you know he is in love with a classmate, some girl from a godforsaken household? Ambika has nobody. She'll come back, don't you worry."

A beguiling, keen, and calculating SriSham remembered every detail and word of every occasion.

His mother narrated the gentleman's behavior toward her and his wife and how Ambika was her daddy's little girl. The father had an engaging and fascinating past.

"Shyam, she expected her husband to be like her dad. There are a few mundane similarities. That may be why Ambika married you. Her father is from the south. He comes from an impoverished family.

He is a self-educated man. She saw that in you since you had the same background. I now have a theory about this. I saw a man with exemplary habits along with love and respect for everyone. This man is a gem! You should have seen the salutes he got from every corner of the grounds on the parade day. I really wish you had been there.

"It shouldn't be difficult for Ambika, with such good and caring people around, to be able to bring your boy up. Shyam, your son will not miss you, not even an iota, not for a second. She has her education, a good job, and most of all, gold in her father and brother not to forget a smart mother and a house full of servants. Your boy will be nothing but a joy for them all. You will be the ONLY loser if you do not act now", The word alienating him, came out emphatically.

"Shyam, do you understand what I'm saying? There's no reason for Ambika to come back to you with such an excellent fallback system and resources, not that even women without such resources would go back to abusive husbands. No woman should."

There it was. She had finally articulated her thoughts. She understood the overt image of her son and had a good glimpse of his covert reality. She had seen it all before.

"Shyam, don't fret or feel inferior. They are good people. They will make you comfortable and will not put you down. Be smart about this. Be honest, apologize sincerely, fall on your father-in-law's feet. If you humble yourself, you might win your wife and son back."

The politically crude and reluctant SriSham flew to Delhi upon his mother's persuasion. He pleaded with Ambika's father and promised exceptional behavior and a gentlemanly attitude from then on. Ambika agreed to go back to Bombay only if her mother came and stayed with them in Bombay, so SriSham got his wife and son back in his life.

The first few months went smoothly. Ambika's father visited them at least once a month on the pretext of having some business to attend to there. Ambika was busy catching up on her work. Her mother's constant complaints about Bombay and its incessant, torrential rains, its slums, and its exorbitant prices for everyday goods such as vegetables tortured SriSham, and his wife's father even said that he could work from his Bombay office if he needed to. To top it all Ambika kept her paychecks to herself without spending a penny for the household expenses. She was clear about the arrangement – that SriSham was the one to take care of all expenses.

She was an emancipated woman in every other sense. But it was the responsibility of the man of house to take care of the household expenses – she argued. SriSham suspected that Ambika's mother constantly advised her to save her earnings separately in a savings account. She voiced her concerns that with his temperament, SriSham could not be trusted for her welfare. SriSham was able to take care of the household. He paid for the rent, the groceries and utilities. All he wanted to know was how much Ambika made and what she did with it. She was secretive about her income. Over everything else, money finally became a very serious point of contention.

His much-awaited relief from Ambika's family came in the shape of her younger brother. He was taking his exams soon, and the duty-bound mother decided to go back to New Delhi. The cook had left on a family emergency for two months, and the young man had his college-related work and had no time for cooking for himself and his father.

"Ahh—finally!" SriSham sighed in relief.

Ambika's mother promised to be back after hiring and training a new cook who would be compatible with her son's and her husband's palates.

Ambika trusted SriSham's kindly mother enough to have her stay with them after her mother's departure. SriSham's mother tended to her son and kept an eye on her's too.

But SriSham's dormant habits came back with his mother's arrival. The taken-for-granted mother took care of the household—cooking, cleaning, babysitting, grocery shopping, knitting shawls for her beautiful daughter-in-law—but she could not control her son's temper.

When SriSham got his free hand back, all his pent-up tumultuousness got the better of him again. He would not be controlled in his own home. His unidentifiable mental conditions and general disrespect for womanhood that came either from the culture or from his family threatened every vulnerable soul around him.

Their fights escalated month by month, and the beatings eventually resumed.

"Mother, tell her it's an honor to be home. She is not helping with the household expenses either. What is the point in her working? Let her stop working and pamper you and the baby at home. I do not want to trouble you at your age with all the responsibilities of caring for a child."

"Shyam, this is not a conundrum for me. Let her continue to work."

Ambika herself was straightforward and made it clear. "My job is my only solace and place of freedom. I won't quit working. With your attitude and spend-thrift aptitude, quitting is very scary" She was unrelenting and persistent; she worked long hours.

His total resentment turned into bitterness, and his mother was voiceless. When she literally got in between them, she received slaps. The mother and the wife were no match for him.

Their nights were engulfed in arguments until Ambika's voice grew shrill.

Their second child was a miracle.

SriSham sent her to Delhi and told her not to come back. She never did.

He's drowning in this flood of events, his mother thought. *Just let it go.*

SriSham's third visit to Ambika's family was an utter failure. The family had moved and had not left a forwarding address. SriSham changed jobs and moved to Delhi hoping to eventually see Ambika and his sons in the area.

Ambika sent him a notice of divorce from Tanjore, at the southern tip of India, a few months after the second birthday of his second son. He had forgotten about their native village.

He went to the courts with his mother. "Boys engage better with their fathers," he yelled as he banged on a desk to harass the court clerks. He had not hired a lawyer; there was no purpose, he said. "It's a clear-cut case of a belligerent, badgering wife. Anyone can easily see how arrogant my wife was in serving me, an engineer, with divorce papers!"

Ambika's family could afford and had gotten the best lawyer in town. SriSham's firstborn got up on the stand and affirmed his intentions to stay with his mother and grandfather. There were no arguments about the second boy. The court ruled that SriSham could come back when the first boy turned twelve and submit another petition for custody, but the second boy would remain with the mother. The logic behind that was that the first son had seen his father and had lived with him, so any attachment he had with his father could be explained.

"I lost my two gems" was SriSham's only comment as he got out on the dusty Chennai streets with his doting and indulgent but sensible mother.

CHAPTER 4

S riSham sent applications to US colleges with MBA programs because his younger brother was then in that country. He thought, *I'm brighter than he is. I scored higher in math in my senior year than he did. I should be the one there now. How did he get there?'*

SriSham received a full scholarship to the MBA program at Ohio State's Fisher College of Business. He left India asking his mother to be on the lookout for a girl to marry in a year or two after he received his green card.

In the years following his divorce, he had lived with a married woman in Chennai and had promised to take her with him when he moved to the United States. But when he did move to the US, he told her that he wanted to get his degree, a green card, and a good job before sponsoring her.

In the United States, he dated women and took them to his apartment but was constantly calling and writing to his mother asking her to find a woman who had never been married.

"After all, mother, everyone wants to marry a green card holder. There shouldn't be any difficulty."

"But Shyam, you don't have a green card yet, and that's not a character certificate."

"I'll marry only after I get it. But you must be on the lookout," he said ignoring her slights.

"But Shyam, they somehow know about the Bharatha Natyam dancer, Kamahi, who lived with you in Columbus for a few months."

"Mother, Kamahi spreads malice. I housed her and her daughter because they were touring the United States and giving performances for the Indian crowd here. She claimed a place to stay when they were here in Columbus, and I let her stay at my place. That's all there was to it."

"Won't the organizers arrange a good family for a woman to stay with when she's by herself with a young daughter in a new country?"

"Well, the organizers were looking for people to house them, and I volunteered."

"Well, she wasn't happy about her stay with you, and she's been quite vocal about it. This small town has come to know so much about my son's virility in Columbus that nobody here will give their daughters' hand in marriage to you." She promised to be on the lookout elsewhere—Bangalore or Chennai, bigger cities where the flock was more open to a daughter marrying a divorcé.

The demands of a master's degree program, a part-time job, an apartment, and chores coupled with not having a driver's license or knowing how to cook made his life difficult. He was older than forty. His idea was not to complete a master's degree; it was to make the US his permanent abode, marry a young woman, and have a son to make up for the two he had lost. He wanted to live a grand life to taunt his brother, Ambika, and her brother, whom he had heard was a surgeon in a hospital near Orlando, Florida.

SriSham's brother gained a green card for him through his employer, a businessman with many small businesses just on the books; SriSham started working for him for a pittance.

His "Foreign boy with a US green card" status did not work no matter how hard SriSham's mother tried to get a girl who had never been married until she found the plain-looking Nirmala, an innocent divorcée with no children. Nirmala was not a college-educated woman, so she met SriSham's first condition. He had told his mother, "No degree holder. Just a high school education; first marriage; definitely not postmenopausal." His mother knew SriSham wanted a child, and she was ecstatic when she found Nirmala. Every one of SriSham's conditions was met except for the fact it would not be her first marriage. "An innocent divorcée with no issues," she had told him.

SriSham went to India for ten days and met Nirmala. He liked her fair skin, long hair, and quiet disposition. They were married within three days. The only attendees at his second marriage were Nirmala's brother and his wife and SriSham's mother. Nirmala had been working after her first marriage had been annulled, and her savings were just about enough to pay for the garland, her wedding outfit, and lunch for five.

SriSham's mother consoled herself: *Well, the first gala wedding didn't work for my son, so maybe this simpler one will.*

Nirmala joined SriSham in the US three months later after receiving a green card. He sent her back to India a couple of times because she was not "behaving," but Nirmala's brother sent her right back after confirming that she was "fine and dandy."

SriSham's mother continued to advise him over the phone. "Shyam," she would start lovingly, "if a woman is arrogant, it affects only herself and her job. But if a man is arrogant, it affects everyone around him and people who come into his life especially his spouse and those who take care of him. If you want to have Nirmala stay in your life, change your attitude."

An irate SriSham would say, "Yes, mother," half-heartedly. His calls to his mother slowly dwindled in number. His kind mother kept asking SriSham's brother to coax him into calling her.

"Do you know mother has not received a call from you in six months? SriSham, she just wants to know how you are. Can't you try to call and speak with her more often?"

"Can't you tell her I'm doing just fine yourself?"

"She wants to hear your voice. No matter how much I try to convince her you're fine, she insists that you call her."

SriSham called his mother and asked her not to speak with his younger brother. "Mother, do you know the FBI is after your favorite, your younger son?"

"Why? What for?"

She didn't sound alarmed to SriSham, so he decided to hype the matter up.

"Do you know he cooked the books of the small firms he was auditing? He helped them hide millions of dollars to avoid taxes. Some of these business owners are political crooks."

His mother knew that her younger son ran a successful CPA firm in Columbus but did not know or understood the details.

Her silence encouraged SriSham. "Mother, why do you think I quit the job at the firm run by one of his clients? I am distancing myself from him. I don't want the FBI to start following me too and start asking me questions or worse—coming to my college and workplace and deny my visa too... Mother, are you there?"

"Yes Shyam, I am very much here." Her disinterest came through. "Your brother is no crook."

Her words suddenly reminded him of the October 1988 debate between Democratic vice-presidential candidate Senator Lloyd Bentsen and Republican vice-presidential candidate Senator Dan Quayle: "Mother, I served with crooks. I know crooks. Some are friends of mine. Mother, he's a crook." SriSham couldn't help but guffaw.

The mother had no context for his joke.

"Mother, if I continued to deal with him, they would send me back to India. I certainly don't want to go back to India. Do you want me back there? Mother, please do not take his calls. Our DSP in Vellore may come to your house to question you. I'm referring to the deputy superintendent of police, Vellore Branch. He knows us all very well through our loving father's magnificent brother."

His mother seemed to come alive. "Shyam, how do you know the FBI is after your brother?"

"The other day, I spoke with my immigration lawyer. He seemed to have some doubts about the firm that sponsored me for the green card. He revealed some details and said that the FBI was investigating some of the cases of the firm, which means the FBI is after your little son, doesn't it?"

"I thought your immigration matter was all over."

"Yes, I have a green card. But if the company that sponsored me is no good, that green card is null and void."

"Can you give me more details about how your little brother is involved? I mean, it's normal for big firms to be dealing with some lawsuits especially in the United States, isn't it?"

"Mother, you're a bright woman, yes, but the details I hear will not make any sense to you. These are complicated business laws, too intense even for an executive MBA from Fisher College." SriSham cackled. "Mother, just remember that he's being followed by the FBI. I wrote in my diary today, 'Wow, my little brother is wanted by the FBI according to my lawyer.' You will find solace in forgetting the rest and know that no amount of your prayers will save him at this juncture. Please do not ask him to come and see me or call me unless you want me to go jail too. And don't ask him anything about it. I have enough problems with him, his wife, the firm, and his lawyers. Don't add fuel to fire."

SriSham had picked up the habit of writing in a diary daily from his father, the only habit akin to those of his maker. He had an eidetic memory, but he found it difficult to remember the Western names that were all around him then. There were too many Jims and Chucks, and their last names were from every part of the world. The spelling of their names did not match their pronunciation, so he had written down his lawyer's name the way it was pronounced in his mother tongue, Tamil, and his phone number as well: "FBI is following my brother—reassured by my lawyer, J ... R ... Esq."

Nirmala called SriSham's mother when he was not home; their frequent chitchatting kept the mother happy. Those calls dwindled when SriSham saw his mother's number on their phone bill, which resulted in his slapping her face.

Nirmal, as SriSham called her, finally became pregnant when SriSham was about to hit fifty. "I know it's a boy," he assured her. "You know I can beget only boys," he said and laughed uncontrollably.

"Please, doctor," he told her obstetrician, "we don't want to know the sex of the baby. I'm not that kind of Indian guy," he assured him. "He'll become a right royal citizen of this wonderful country the minute he enters this world. He'll grow up to be a lucky man," SriSham said smiling.

He came up with a list of boys' names. "How about Srivatsa, Sriram, Srikar, or Srihan?" he asked his wife. "There's really no word in English for the Sanskrit *sri* or for that matter in any other language. This one Sanskrit word can never be translated into any language because its meaning is endless," he boasted.

"How about some girls' names?" Nirmala asked.

"Let's not wear ourselves out. It's going to be a boy I'm a hundred percent sure."

"The hospital wants two names, one for a male and one for a female child."

"Okay, then, how about Mandodhari, the demon's wife in Ramayana?" SriSham's boisterous guffaw was new and uncontrollable; his eyes were watering. His nostrils were flaring.

"That's not funny. I'm going to name her Lakshmi."

"No, it's Rashmi."

"What would we call her, Rash, Rashy?"

"No, just *mi mi mi mi mi mi* ..." SriSham sang and went around Nirmala as he laughed.

Nirmala had their daughter at the university hospitals a week before the due date.

"What a travesty!" was all SriSham could come up with. "She should have been a boy!" He could not accept the fact that he was the father of a daughter. He was wise enough not to lament about it outwardly knowing he was in the United States. He was often seen consoling his wife not to worry because he could bring her up like an excellent boy worthy of everyone's envy. He wanted her to attend Harvard or Yale, or Oxford or Cambridge, or go to India and take all the tests to gain a seat in the prestigious collage referred as I.I.T (Indian Institute of Technology). Before heading home with the infant, Nirmala had urged her doctors to perform a tubal ligation since SriSham did not care for accidents, and with his obsession with a son, there was no telling as to what was going on in his mind.

Nirmala was engrossed in her vivacious newborn. She struggled with SriSham's quixotic career; he quit jobs generally after just six months.

"Our job is the same," she told him, "whether we have a boy or a girl. Our duty is to feed our baby, change her diapers, send her to good schools, and save for college as well as providing a decent household. Would it be any different or easy if she were a boy? Would he survive without food for two days just because he was a boy?" She rationalized the way she knew.

SriSham's ambivalence, his own curiosity and love, Nirmala's argument, seemed to influence SriSham's attitude. It was amusing to see the way he obsessed with the infant's care.

He became involved. He would bathe her with the finest soap and shampoo. Cleaned up the tub obsessively before her bath. He had new towels ready sitting on a side-table outside the bathroom. He dressed her up and laid her on the softest pillow to carry her;

he said his hands were too bony for her comfort. He cuddled her, bottle-fed her, gazed into her eyes, and cooed perfect English words. He rocked her in a new rocking chair, sterilized everything before she touched it including his hands and her pacifiers, made silly faces for her entertainment, and played peekaboo with her. He helped her graduate from milk to baby food including a variety of fruits and vegetables. Rashmi always had a kempt little coif on her head. He even adopted the name Nirmala used while addressing her!

His indifference to her turned into compassion for her. He tried to make her into his own self; he questioned everything Nirmala suggested for their daughter, and he made sure Rashmi always had the best of the best.

The first couple of times SriSham lost his job, Nirmala did not ask for anything, but later, she became blunt and talked back to him without any hesitation since he was slowly mellowing down even though occasionally he yelled at her and slapped her. He lost one job right after their daughter's second birthday. His home stays were always the same—constant nagging for a foot massage and constant requests for hot water or Horlicks.

One time when he was home for a few days, she mustered her strength and asked him pointedly, "Are you taking some time off, or have you lost your job again?"

"That bitch, that devil of the female @#*&% said I misplaced customers' checks all the time. She stole the checks that were deposited. My accounts were perfect. Customers were very happy with me. That a$#^% couldn't stand my guts."

Such answers became his standard reply.

"You know my friend Nandhini, don't you?" Nirmala asked.

SriSham had seen her at parties for people from India.

"She's been asking if I could cook for her. She and her husband are working and then attending school in the evening. They're working on master's degrees."

SriSham liked people who studied, especially those going after master's degrees. His silence encouraging her.

"She said she would come to pick up what I cook for them. She knows I don't drive. She'll pay me well, you know. You call them DINKS—double income no kids."

"So, you think I won't get another job?" SriSham was angry as well as dejected.

"No. I'd do the cooking only until you get another job. The last time you lost your job—"

She could not complete her sentence. SriSham interrupted it with a hard slap to her face.

She started wailing; she raced for the door and ran down the hallway. It looked as though she stood closer to the front door during their conversations all prepared to dart out. There was this innate preparedness or intuition to save herself while SriSham was around. She was more familiar and friendly with her neighbors than she was with him. Someone opened an apartment door to see what the commotion was all about, and Nirmala ran into the apartment by reflex.

"I'm calling the cops," the neighbor said and turned to the phone.

"Please don't! This happens rarely these days—you know that. We'll work it out, so please don't."

As fate would have it, another neighbor had already called the police. SriSham was leaving the apartment when two policemen showed up at his door.

"We got a call from your neighbors, sir. Are you SriSham Venka ... ta ... chalam?"

"Yes I am." SriSham said "What's wrong, officer? Everything's fine with us. My wife and I had a small argument, and she ran out. She's quite dramatic you know."

"Sir, where's your wife?" The policeman was stern.

Just then, Nirmala walked in still wearing just her slip, which she slept in. A towel went wrapping around her shoulders. Her neighbor had given her the towel to stop her shivering and to wipe her face and runny nose. "No, nothing happened, sir," she said. "We'll make sure not to disturb our neighbors again." Looked like she had learned to speak decent English.

The policemen stood there at their doorstep for a few minutes. Nirmala explained the situation, slap and everything. None of the neighbors came out. They wanted nothing to do with the matter;

they couldn't take time off for court hearings as witnesses. They were not comfortable with SriSham at all; they had seen him get into fights at the drug store a few times when he was refilling his prescription.

He had complained to the druggist, "My date of birth is not mandatory to refill my prescription. It's illegal to ask for birthdays."

"Just your date of birth, sir, not the year. It makes it easier to find your refills because it's unique."

"My name is unique enough in this part of the world. Just look for my last name. I'll spell my last name for you. It starts with a V"—he had ignored the druggist's exasperated expressions — "and e, n, k, a, and t. Venkat means precious jewel."

The oddity had uneased the druggist and the on-lookers.

One of the policemen said, "If this happens again, your husband will go to jail." The cops glared at SriSham and his wife and left.

After that incident, SriSham quieted down. He started looking for jobs in states far away from Ohio; he was not a happy camper there during the winter. Florida was warm, but Ambika's successful surgeon brother lived there. Texas looked like a vibrant place with warm weather and inexpensive housing. He was applying for jobs while Nirmala was cooking for Nandhini and a whole slew of immigrants who were busy working, studying, partying—things young people in a new country enjoyed doing.

Indian movies were screened at the Upper Arlington Library

theater. Nirmala went there with fresh *samosas* and *pakoras* and thermoses of hot chai; she made a considerable amount of money during intermissions. When they moved the screenings to the university theatre, they rented an adjacent kitchen, so Nirmala could make fresh *chaat papree*. Moviegoers would throng her kitchen during intermissions, and some came in to just eat her goodies when the movies were lousy.

Nirmala cooked and learned north and south Indian curries. The lingering curry smell in their apartment and on her clothes kept SriSham away. Nirmala asked SriSham to take care of Rashmi when she was busy cooking, and he did so without a fuss. She was busy cooking for her customers, who would come by in the evenings to pick up their favorite dinners, and he was applying for jobs in Texas while he wasn't caring for Rashmi and buying her the best outfits, changing her diapers, and feeding her. He read to her incessantly. He was a constant presence in her life, and Nirmala was happy that SriSham was happy.

SriSham heard those coming to pick up food saying, "You know Nirmal Aunty—she runs their family. They have a little kid, and she can't drive, so it's critical that we help her." And at university gatherings, he was known not as SriSham but as Nirmala's husband.

SriSham decided to move out of Columbus as soon as he could.

CHAPTER 5

The move to Houston was a cinch. The human resources department of his new employer found him a great apartment. They came with their meager belongings that had fit into one small moving van. SriSham was proud that his company took care of him. He told Nirmala to quit her catering business; his job paid him sufficiently. He laid down the law—she should never cook for anyone other than him and their daughter and that no visitors were allowed in their apartment without his knowledge. After all, he was starting a brand-new life with a squeaky-clean slate in Houston.

It was Nirmala who introduced him to her saint; she showed him a photo of him. "I'm interested in enlarging this picture of my angel to forty by forty-five inches."

"Are you crazy?" her asked her. "Do you have any idea how big it would be? We don't have room in this tiny place for such a big picture of your *holiness*." SriSham's did not hide his irritation.

"I've measured this wall. It's bare, and there's enough room."

"Just who *is* this quaint saint? I wonder why you have his photo everywhere in our home and in your purse. Surely, he's not feeding you or giving you those exotic jewels you're saving for Rashmi."

Nirmala had been saving for their daughter the Indian way. People paid an Indian jeweler in Houston one hundred dollars a month for a lottery system; the winner gets to buy gold for three thousand dollars right away but will sign a contract to pay one hundred dollars for thirty months, and Nirmala had won it once.

"Surely, he will give you anything and everything you want in life under the sun and above the sky and stars," he said mocking her.

She was confident in her answer. "You know, we should go to the temple they've built for this great saint in Houston."

"There's no dearth of Hindu temples in Houston. There's a new one opening every month—nothing but big business and enough politics to go with it."

SriSham could not be persuaded – well – just in the beginning.

"Well, let me challenge you," she said. "You say you've been waiting for Eric, your coworker, to retire so that you can apply for his position because you know his job inside out."

"In and out," he said to correct her.

"Yes, yes. You come with me to the new temple I just told you about and ask him to make Eric think seriously about retiring and see for yourself if Eric retires tomorrow or not", enthusiastically adding, "You can even pray for that job right away without asking for Eric to retire, and you'll get some encouraging news about it tomorrow!"

She had been asking him to pray to this chosen person for years; she thought this could be SriSham's lucky break. She wanted to go to the temple, but she needed him to drive her there; he insisted that she not learn how to drive and that no one else could drive her anywhere. He had started a new life in Houston, and he didn't want her blabbering mouth to ruin things for him.

"I will accept your challenge," he said vehemently.

SriSham took her to the temple and saw the throng of people. He was puzzled at first at this world of saints, god-men, preachers, gurus, and others.

Eric did retire, something he had been planning, and SriSham was promoted to his position. His salary went up, and he got a fancy nameplate for his desk. Emails announced his promotion to everyone in the company. Some congratulated him through another email. He was more than pleased to move up in his work! Nothing could enthrall him more!

"I still don't have the type of job I'm capable of handling. After all, I'm an engineer with an executive MBA you see," he bragged to Nirmala and to a handful of new friends in Houston.

Nirmala gave him a book of stories about her saint that were ancient. "If you read this book every day, you'll get any job you desire."

"Does everyone who belongs to your illustrious group read this book?" he asked. After all, her saint had given him the promotion.

"No, that's the problem. Nobody does though it's been translated into all languages under the sun. They say you'll get everything you want if you read the book regularly."

That caught his interest; after all, his desires were many. He definitely wanted a house bigger than Ambika's brother's house, which he had googled, and he was following him on Facebook as well. Nothing short of a miracle would give him that lifestyle. He also wanted his two sons to shun Ambika and come live with him. He had once showed up at the doctor's door suspecting his two sons were there. The doctor had called the cops on him and then served him with a restraining order. SriSham's anger knew no bounds but violating the restraining order would involve criminal charges. His mother insisted she didn't know the whereabouts of her two grandsons in India.

He had thought Ambika's brother was a surgeon, but then he discovered he was just a family practitioner, and that made him happy and less envious. He told his mother about this thinking she would listen to his ramblings on the matter, but she brushed him aside; she said family practitioners were the frontline soldiers, warriors who had the awesome responsibility of diagnosing patients' illnesses and referring them to the appropriate specialists. SriSham stopped broaching the subject.

"So, what does attending services at the temple require?" he asked Nirmala. He was hoping that going there once a month would be sufficient and easy if it resulted in more rewards for him.

She settled for a monthly trip after arguing for weekly trips, but it didn't take too long until they were going weekly. He bought English translations of all the books in the temple bookstore that mentioned anything about his piety.

The two were reading about the same saint though in different languages; she quoted from the book when he committed the slightest infraction, and that would silence him. He considered it sacrilegious to go against a written word. He had the utmost respect for all written words. Also, he was fearful of getting sacked at work.

"The new manager isn't that happy with my work," he told her one evening.

"Just read the book aloud." She knew the solutions for all his problems. "He will hear you."

He read it, and his type A personality urged him to talk about stories he had read about the saint. At first, he read the book to children every Sunday in the temple's classrooms. The children needed to be as innocent and trusting as possible to sit through the stories, but they were. No one read it like he did. His English was flawless. He made silly jokes for children. And he was always prepared for the class.

He had some large posters with the virtuoso's picture in the center and his face showing up at the bottom corner with the time and date of his classes. He called himself the mystic SriSham who had known the saint during his previous seven lives, and he called his classes discourses.

His lectures were free as his posters pronounced in bold letters along with, "Sumptuous lunch served after the discourse." His wife had insisted on that because free food drew people everywhere in the world, and she would prepare the meals.

He printed the posters at a famous poster center and distributed the posters to temples saying he had them from his earlier narratives of thirty-plus years. He said he had just changed the venue, the time, the date and his picture. "In those days, I charged heavily for my narratives," he would say, "but not anymore. I have enough wealth. I decided it was time to take my saint to the world free of charge. Do you know these swamis who come to Houston from India? They charge you what you make in a month or what your wives make in six months (his crowds liked him saying that their salaries were six times greater than their wives' salaries) just to rationalize for an hour. Not me. I introduce you to our saint at no cost to you."

He hung the posters in the room where they had shoe racks and coat hangers. The temples ran them on their website upon SriSham's advice. It was important to him that Ambika, her brother, and his sons saw them. Like Iago says to Cassio in Shakespeare's Othello, SriSham did not realize that his reputation was without merit.

Nirmala cooked for the gatherings in the temple kitchen in the beginning; Rashmi attended the classes her father taught. Children and adults had a blast eating fried *pooris* after the class and served with *chana masala* and sweet *chum-chums* one Sunday and then saffron pilaf and vegetable *korma* with *savion kheer* the next. Without fail, there were appetizers—*samosas* and *pakoras* with *dhokla*. For those on diets, there was *masala chai* and *mango lassi*. Later, the devotees turned the Sunday classes into pot-luck lunches since the crowd was too much for a single cook to handle. SriSham enjoyed the variety of dishes.

All children's classes invariably ended with the children touching the feet of the teacher and touching those fingers to their closed eyes, chest, or head. "They must learn our culture, you know," SriSham would say. The parents demonstrated for their children how they were to fall on SriSham's feet head first or bend to touch his feet and then touch their eyes, chin, or chest. Also, it all depended on availability of time. If they had time to spare after the class, they fell onto his feet and got up. If they were in a rush, they just bent down extending their right hand in the direction of SriSham's feet (not necessitating to touch them) and hurriedly brought the fingers up to touch either their eyes, chin, chest or heads, "After all, children are great mimics you know," he would say. "They know only what we do."

The young mothers were all beautiful, and some were professionals. The fathers were very well educated and had good jobs or professions. SriSham loved it when a doctor or a surgeon would fall at his feet.

The more progressive of the devotees and those who could not bow due to back-pain gave SriSham hugs instead of falling on his feet, and some just shook his hand, but SriSham was averse to hugs.

Hugs made him cringe. He had never hugged anyone in all his sixty years; that would have necessitated a definite integrality of the use of an antiperspirant.

"Children, it's best to touch the feet of your parents, teachers, and saints. That act of complete and egoless surrender makes them bless you from the bottom of their hearts with everything you want in life. I am flattered to teach you that complete surrender. Wipe away your egos since they are our first and foremost enemies."

Such teachings still did not deter a number of them from giving SriSham hugs after class. SriSham would cringe and move a step away when anyone came near him.

Nirmala knew he was very uneasy in that respect. "Let's stop by the Indian boutique on Arne Street," she said when they were leaving the temple one afternoon after a big pot-luck lunch.

"Not sari buying again, Nirmala. You got a few last month."

"No, this time it's for you. Just take me to Arne Street. I'll show you."

She bought him three shawls—shiny orange, sky blue, and yellow—with Om printed on them. Once he draped them over his shoulders and around his neck, he saw that he looked like the saint sitting on the pedestal of the temple. The resemblance stunned him. *She's brilliant!* he thought.

"Once you look like their saint, no one will dare come near you," Nirmala said with a smile.

It was not the practice of commoners to touch a saint. It started as a religious and socioeconomic practice of the untouchables in India. Anyone wearing a yellow shawl was generally beyond the grasp of commoners. (but the slippery material would not stay on his shoulders during his multi-hour ramblings that he kept adjusting the shawl. He put a sticky-note to himself '*do not forget to bring binder clips from work*' to keep the shawl on his shoulders)

Everything else became inconsequential to SriSham. Children, women, and men swarmed around him and fell at his feet every week. His wife and daughter were not just another woman and child in the temple; they belonged to this great soul. Nirmala stayed in the teacher's hall. After the lecture, she would walk slowly to the dining hall. A table was always set ready for the three of them. The devotees packed up leftovers for SriSham and stuffed the bags that Nirmala had brought for that purpose.

"This is indeed a blessed temple," people were saying. "Our kids' teacher lived with our saint in a number of his past lives."

Some people invited SriSham to come to their homes to bless them. They would invite every Hindu they knew to show their position in the community and their close involvement with their saint's deputy. SriSham said he himself was the saint due to his association with him during his past lives; those who were skeptical about that left, but many remained. And there was always a new crowd—mothers visiting their daughters who were about to give birth or who had given birth. SriSham made it a point to bless the newborns. The sixty- and seventy-year-olds from India sat patiently not following a word as SriSham lectured on House Speaker Nancy Pelosi and Google's Sundhar Picchai to the host's one-month-old baby. Some became his ardent devotees mainly because they understood nothing of what he said but recognized the name from the TV news.

SriSham's diatribes did not appeal to everyone; many made it a point to come to these lectures after SriSham's lecture was over. They called it outrageous. While thirty or so would listen to him, there would be fifty or so who would line up to pay their respects to him. SriSham had made it a rule that no one could go into the dining room until they had all prostrated themselves in front of him and had received some flower petals from him. "Devotees cannot eat before getting blessings. Gluttons are not allowed in my prayer session. To show that you had been blessed, show your plastic bag in the dining room with the shredded blooms. That is your passport," he said with a laugh, and others laughed with him.

SriSham wanted the video to show a long line of people waiting to cast themselves face down on his feet in utter humility and especially touching his feet and then their eyes or head. Every one of the devotees stayed and pitched ideas and paid tribute to him for a few minutes. SriSham enjoyed making everyone in the line wait for him. After all, he would be the last one to eat.

If you cut in line and went straight to the trays where the frazzled forget-me-nots were kept, you were in dire danger—SriSham would catch you and make you go the end of the line.

Invariably, his daughter, Rashmi, would be the first one to submit to him, get one full yellow rose, and be the first one to eat as she was the *devi*, the female goddess of the program. While four- and five-year-olds were made to wait until ten p.m. to eat, he had *masala chai* and hot water constantly throughout the discourse. And when the line formed, he sipped chai, left the cup with the host standing nearby, dropped petals on the ones at his feet, posed for photos, and made wisecracks. He called those who did not attend the discourse rats for whom there was no salvation in this birth and in the seven to come.

He also took the envelope the host gave him. In it would be three hundred dollars to four hundred dollars depending on the crowd. The host usually sent an envelope around after the discourse, and everyone contributed a Lincoln or a Hamilton. He rarely saw a Franklin or a Grant though there were quite a number of Washingtons.

He made sure the video was cut and put away after everyone fell at his feet. He insisted that the envelope be given to him when he was ready to leave for the evening after dinner tucked in a plate along with some fruits and coconuts. After this platter was given to him by the hosts, they would fall on his feet together and that was the traditional way to perform obeisance to their mentor, their teacher, their priest.

CHAPTER 6

SriSham's jeremiads were getting bolder. So was his friendship with the camera woman, Emma. One evening after the discourse, SriSham was giving geraniums as people were falling on his feet one by one. As they got up, he said a few words to them and asked a select few to stand beside him; he asked Emma to take a photo. There was a long line in front of him of about forty devotees.

On the other side of the family room near the dining room were two students from Rice University in tight jeans posing for Emma, whose back was to SriSham. Her long, brown hair was braided and had strands of jasmine in it. SriSham found that irresistible; he left the line and walked toward Emma and the jean-clad students. He brushed hard against Emma from behind and without flinching continued to walk toward the girls.

SriSham laughed and joked with the girls for a few minutes while the gathering patiently waited for him to come back to his original spot. He did not care about the young children who were waiting in line with their parents. The delay was inexcusable to those in line, and as they were driving home, Nirmala pointed that out. Of late, she had been worried about his behavior toward Emma.

"You know there were children waiting in line to prostrate themselves and receive your blessings. They could eat only after they did that and got flowers from you. Why did you leave the line to talk to those jean-clad girls while devotees were waiting in line?"

SriSham was driving, Rashmi was in the front passenger seat, and Nirmala was in the back seat behind Rashmi. Making such a comment from the back seat with Rashmi there was the safest time for her to do so, as Nirmala had come to believe.

SriSham was driving in the right lane at thirty-five miles an hour on a side road where the speed limit was forty-five miles an hour. He avoided the highways because other motorists would honk at him for going so slowly, race past him, and give him the finger. Hence, he avoided driving on the highways at any cost.

SriSham's having left his post and his stealthy attitude toward Emma hurt Nirmala, but she did not mention that in front of Rashmi. That was the second time that had happened. SriSham did not talk much to Nirmala those days unless she threw questions at him. He answered her patiently when Rashmi was around.

Rashmi had mentioned her father's behavior toward her mother to her school counselor, and the counselor had asked SriSham to attend a session with her. Nirmala went by herself. The hesitant and vigilant SriSham, given to keeping his own counsel, refused.

"Rashmi, the counselee knowns more than the counselor. Ask your teacher to come to me if she wants to say anything to me." After all, he was counseling the world.

Rashmi's counselor indeed showed up at his tiny apartment one afternoon after school.

"My, what a surprise. Please come in," Nirmala said as she beamed at the visitor.

Mrs. Moore told SriSham that she wanted to talk with him for ten minutes. She told him her job was to take care of her students whatever was troubling them.

SriSham did not like her. But after her visit, SriSham stayed away from Nirmala as much as he could especially when Rashmi was around. His only regret about the teacher's visit was that he had not cleaned up his desk, which had piles of newspapers towering to the ceiling, a dictionary, a thesaurus, things he had printed out in reams and reams of paper, a few mousetraps, cereal boxes, stack of overdue library books, marks left by coffee cups, disinfectant wipes, pens, highlighters, lottery tickets, receipts—it looked like the lost-and-found room in a department store.

Nirmala, seated behind Rashmi in their old station-wagon, could not stop.

"There's no cause for you to leave the line until everyone gets a dining ticket, those bags with petals and blessings from you. Emma will not send anyone home without taking his or her picture with you. You don't have to worry about going to the devotees to have a picture taken."

"Can you stop your rambling? You can have your say about it once we reach home."

That shut her up then, but that night after Rashmi went to bed, Nirmala brought the matter up again.

"I wanted to bring to your attention not just leaving the line but watching out. You know Emma's husband does our videos. You don't want him to see things when he replays and edits them like I could see with plain eyes. Emma's children are in your discourses too. You should be conscious of others watching your actions."

SriSham's anger knew no bounds.

"What the hell?" He grabbed her big bun of hair and dragged her to the floor from the bed on which she was seated. She wailed as her back hit the floor. SriSham got on top of her, pressed her open left palm with his right knee trying to break it and before she could get another sound out, he covered her face with a pillow he snatched off the bed. She was trying to shove him off with her right hand when both heard Rashmi's room door open and her anklets rushing towards their bedroom. SriSham quickly got up and sat on the bed with legs crossed like a saint. He closed his eyes. His palms were resting on his knees with a symbolic *mudra*; He assumed a yogic posture.

Nirmala sat up on the floor; her bun was disheveled, and she was holding her contoured left-hand writhing in pain, the hand SriSham had been kneeling on.

"Mom! What happened? I thought you fell down or something. I heard your freakish yell."

"Yes, Lakshmi, I did. I'm fine. I must have fallen off the bed. I was seated at the edge and must have dozed off. You just go back to bed … Just … go back. You have a lot of school work tomorrow." Rashmi looked at her father seated on the bed in deep meditation.

He definitely had something to do with her yelling, Rashmi thought. *I'll tell Mrs. Moore about this on Monday.*

Rashmi was about sixteen. She was exceptionally tall like SriSham, and she wore her hair in a short bob. The perpetual sadness on her face spoke volumes. Her mother had never seen her smile in the last few years, and she wondered why her daughter was constantly melancholy and sullen. SriSham's threats about her grades could be one reason, she concluded. Mrs. Moore herself had indicated she was in a constant worry mode.

"Rashmi, you'll never get into Harvard or Yale or even Georgia Tech with these kinds of grades," SriSham would tell her. "Look at other Indian kids, spelling bee and geography bee champions and whatnot. What's come over you? Are you distracted? Do you have any boyfriends who don't want you to succeed? Why are you doing this to me? Are you trying to please someone by not getting good grades? What do you do at home after four in the afternoon? Is your mom letting you go to parties these rich Indian kids have all the time to find a rich husband? What has come over you?"

She had had no qualms about yelling back at him at the top of her voice until a neighbor complained about the noise. After that, she started just walking away from him.

"My grades are As and Bs. Have I ever failed a subject?"

"Fail? Now don't you dare report to me about failing. You know I cannot accept anything other than As. When I was in school and college—"

"I know. You sure were a stellar student. Your teachers wrote on your papers that the examinee knew more than the examiner, and they have a mathematics paper of yours in the museum of the city of your birth." Rashmi finished his sentence mockingly and left the room.

SriSham would sometimes follow Rashmi to her room only to be stopped by Nirmala.

"Now, now—she's doing very well in school. You know I attend all her parent-teacher conferences. Her teachers have nothing but good to say about her. Now leave her and her grades alone. If you interfere much, her grades will only go down. Maybe she would do that just to vex you. Don't threaten a teenager. You'll be the loser."

Deja vu; his mother had told him several years earlier, "Shyam, you will be the loser."

SriSham retreated.

Rashmi's closeness to her mother made him vindictive; in his mind, Nirmala was the clear culprit. Mom and her little chum went shopping together and laughed in sync. They had photos taken of themselves in matching ethnic outfits. Jealously drove his animus. His heart was steeped in grudge. *She's pushing our daughter away from me. She's the reason we are always at loggerheads.*

Resorting to bribery, SriSham offered her two yellow roses to come to his discourses, but Rashmi wouldn't budge. She said she was anthophobic.

"What's anthophobic? I know the entire corpus of Shakespeare and have not come upon that word."

"It's a rare malady, Daddy—fear of flowers especially when their filaments are fleeced, slaughtered."

Her excuses for not going varied, some of them mundane, "I have tests tomorrow." "I'm still working on my assignment." "Cannot come to the discourse." "No, Dad, it's not cool to compel me." "You cannot expect me to attend all your rantings," the last word swallowed. Her teenage vehemence came out unhinged.

Her refusals drowned his spirit, but SriSham had once asked her to spell a word in his discourse in front of everyone, and she hadn't liked being put in the limelight. On the occasions she did go to his harangues, she stayed on the second floor of the host's home feigning one or another reading assignment and played with the children who had been sent there.

SriSham did not like young children disturbing his exquisite time. If he heard an infant crying, his face would twitch, and he would stop his descants. Any disturbance distracted and angered him; his eyes and head would jerk around bizarrely. He was easily given to misophonia and would go into a rage. "Why can't the parents control their children as our saint controls us?" he had lamented once, so devotees with infants stayed in another room or came just for dinner.

SriSham had been accompanying groups of his devotees to Kailash, the abode of Shiva. He wanted to keep up with all the infamous and rich swamis of India. He refused Nirmala's pleadings to accompany him; he told her that women could not go to Kailash because it was too sacred a place. When she said that other women in her circle had visited the place, he insisted that it was his philosophy and karmic theory that women should not go with him to Kailash.

However, SriSham entrusted all the prep work for the trips to Nirmala and lectured to her convincingly that helping others get to Kailash fetched more good karma than going there. She booked all the tickets and made every single arrangement for classes for breathing exercises, yoga time at fitness centers, doctors' prescriptions, cooking and packing dry food items, and every errand.

It was Emma's jest that seeded the wondrous idea in SriSham. One evening when they were alone after all the devotees had received the bags of flower petals and were eating, she asked him, "Why don't you take her to Kailash ... and leave her there?" She chuckled and winked. SriSham laughed so hard that all his devotees turned to scrutinize their master and his photographer.

"Now now, it's not that great a joke," Emma said loudly.

SriSham was silent in their drive back home and was quiet for many days after that.

He finally agreed to take Nirmala to Kailash.

"Entertain a tight adherence to rules about fasting," he continually told her, and Nirmala obliged unconditionally. She wanted nothing more than a trip to Kailash.

A month before their journey, SriSham noticed that Nirmala had lost about thirty-five pounds. The rest was easy.

★★★★★

Rashmi and her counselor, Mrs. Moore, came to the police station on August 31. During SriSham's weeklong stay in the prison, they did not allow him to just peer through a blurry cell window day after day but conducted many tests and took him to a prison counselor. His test results revealed that his thirty-plus years of untreated borderline personality disorder was turning slowly but surely into schizophrenia.

The doctor had a chat with the daughter and counselor. "His personality disorder condition has been going on for a long time, but his adamant character has something to do with this too. He has an idiosyncratic belief or impression that he firmly maintained throughout his answers, the fallacy that he's some sort of saint.

That could be a different issue. But he's very delusional and could be schizophrenic. We'll have to test for that. Make an appointment with his primary care physician to get the tests done. I've written prescriptions for now."

He showed medical reports to Mrs. Moore that spelled out that SriSham thought he was the saint. The physician's report said his condition could be manageable if he took the medications and attended counseling.

Drained and humiliated, SriSham got in Mrs. Moore's car. Overcome by desolation and emptiness, he fell into his dark mental dungeon.

His imbecilic desire to continue his second-Saturday floggings sounded preposterous to the crowd. And the kindly prison doctor's advice went unheeded due to his general lack of respect for doctors and their counsel.

By the time Rashmi graduated from high school, SriSham was fully schizophrenic. While scrutinizing his hoarded emails, Rashmi learned of SriSham's brother in Ohio, and Mrs. Moore encouraged her to contact him. He seemed reasonable; he promised to help them if they moved to Ohio; he said that the elevated Medicaid system available in Ohio could help SriSham.

When Rashmi met her uncle for the first time in eighteen years, he was very apologetic. He looked more assimilated, she thought, than were her father and many devotees she was accustomed to in Houston.

"Rashmi, my child, I never for once thought of my brother as a charlatan, I mean, a cheat. He had always been sick, but he refused treatment or counseling. If I had broached that topic with him, his rage would have killed me."

Rashmi said she understood the word, the situation and her father. She still thought he could have tried asking her father to seek counseling at least for his uncontrollable anger, something simpler such as an anger-management class.

"It's also a good thing that your father didn't accept a penny from anyone from a legal point of view. Whatever they gave him, a hundred here or two hundred there, is never a problem. Just focus on yourself from now on. Rashmi, I was worried about you and your wonderful mother. I blundered greatly by not contacting you. I had always suspected my brother was a little off, but I didn't relay that to you. I thought your smart mother would have figured it out." He sounded truly sad. "I do have one piece of advice for you. While it's important to be compassionate with people with health problems such as your father, you must safeguard your own interests especially since you're very young and have your whole life ahead of you. Your father and I are at the fag-end of our lives. Let's do our best but not become overwhelmed about this. Study well, and get a great job, and most important, try to be happy. Keep in touch with Mrs. Moore. Let the distance not deter you. Go and see her whenever you can."

Rashmi came and worked for a year in Columbus, so she could get in-state tuition at Ohio State. SriSham stayed in a well-lit, new, one-room cooperative in a rehabilitation center on Morse Road. When Rashmi visited him one time, he was watching the up-and-coming Hurricane Michael over the Florida panhandle in the reception room.

"Dad," Rashmi said, "Why don't you watch *Are You Being Served* or some British comedy that you love in your room?"

SriSham ignored that; he asked, "Did you get me *palak panner* and garlic *naan* for dinner as I asked?"

"Yes, Dad. I'll take them to your room refrigerator. We can have some snacks there for now, quietly, at your dining table, shall we?"

After the snack and watching an OSU/Indianapolis football home game with him for half an hour, she stood. "Dad, I have to leave before the game ends. The traffic's horrendous once the game crowd heads home."

"Rashmi, your skirt should be slightly longer."

Her six-foot self, seemed mostly legs.

"I'm fine." She was cross. "This is early fall, Dad."

"Your mother was always in a sari. She went to bed wearing a sari.

She wouldn't change into a long nightgown even on hot Houston nights."

"And that was somehow very virtuous?"

There's no winning with this girl, SriSham thought hoping to change the subject. "You know your mother scurried to get garlic *naan* and *paneer* after every discourse from the host's home much to my dislike."

"Dad, they gave them to Mom because they knew you liked those dishes."

"What happened to my devotees, all sixty-five of them?"

"Dad, it's a misnomer. They were just people".

"Ok. Agreed. They were in centers all over the world? Why am I not giving my discourse on second Saturdays?"

"Dad, again, there were no devotees."

"They enjoyed my jokes, didn't they? Didn't they say my humor was top-notch? Didn't they say I was better than Seth Meyers and Jimmy Fallon?"

"Dad, you were the one who said that. Your jokes were all mother-in-law jokes, and all those ladies laughed because that seemed to be the only thing they understood."

"Mother-in-law jokes are funny."

"No, they're not, Dad. Have you ever spent any time with your elderly mother or mother-in-law? Have you ever cared for them as they got older?"

"All of them are dead and gone now, so even if you asked me to, I couldn't," SriSham said trying to joke with Rashmi.

Rashmi was not amused. "Exactly. Remember when grandma was flying in one summer and wanted to spend it in Ohio and then move to Houston during Ohio's winter? You insisted that she come to you in Houston first. Why did you vex her like that?"

"Because I'm the oldest son, the firstborn. She should come to me first."

"Why does it matter? It was just your arrogance. You have to say just the opposite of what everyone says. That made you think you were some sort of an intellectual. Mrs. Moore says the human journey is about developing a heart with eternal love and a mind full of compassion. Once the human race achieves that, we will have achieved everything."

"I know what she said. It's soulful to hear. But that's all it is."

"Everything else is for survival, she says."

Rashmi persistently argued with him about Indian saints and mothers and grandmothers to keep him in check and to get the truth from him regarding her mother. SriSham himself talked a lot about his late wife. He seemed to miss her loyalty and idealism.

"Don't believe any of those who call themselves saints, mystics, and whatnot."

"Then why do you?" she asked.

SriSham tried to change the subject. "Do you have to leave right away? It's only four. Your mother would never have left me alone in this situation. Whatever happened to 'in sickness and in health'?"

"Dad, that dictum is in the context of marriage, for spouses. You know that. Yes, Mom would have stayed with you day in and day out and would have done an excellent job taking care of you. You and I aren't lucky enough to have her with us anymore".

Rashmi continued after a pause "Dad, you'll see your brother on Tuesday, and I'll be back here on Saturday. You'll be just fine. You always said that you don't have a past and future, that you were beyond time, so don't worry about it."

"You're laughing at me."

"Nope. It's all your idea. You can text me for any of your comforts. Bye for now, Dad."

She hurried out without a hug. She stopped at the nurse's station to leave her standard request that his nurses stay with SriSham at medication time until he actually swallowed his tablets.

When her uncle expressed his appreciation for her keeping her dad sane, she said, "I bear with him, Uncle. I want to find out the truth about my mother's so-called death."

STORY 2

Many Me Too

Whatever you do will be insignificant
But it is important that you do it;
In a gentle way you can shake the world

—Mohandas K. Gandhi (1869–1948)

Nellie and Ruma found themselves again at their makeshift headquarters the two teenagers had established for themselves. The comrades had crept up the iron ladder to a cement platform that supported a water tank after the moon had risen. They sprayed the area with mosquito repellent; the spray overpowered the slight odor coming from below.

The two heard the chimes from the cathedral on Nehru Road striking eight o'clock. They were there at their usual spot and usual time. A steam engine was pulling a train through the nearby North Coimbatore station.

Does one's heart calm down if one is seated on a terrace in moonlight? Apparently not. The teenagers' platform was about four or five stories above balconies strewn with potted plants and plastic chairs. They saw a few balconies that had been blocked off with grillwork to make sure miscreants could not break in. They saw screens on windows to keep out the mosquitoes that could bite like piranhas. A heavily-used cricket pitch sat between the buildings and the legs of the water tank. The water tank stood by itself away from the buildings.

The slab was not cordoned off, nor was there a wall as was customary to keep young children from falling off if they got up there. The flat owners were constantly complaining about it to their homeowners' association, but they were told to keep their urchins off the five-story structure themselves.

The space below the slab, which was supported by concrete columns, was full of trash. The locals used the place as a garbage dump though there was a sign declaring 'No Rubbish' in Tamil, the state language, and in English, a language that those who didn't know considered much more official. Ruma and Nellie put up posters that told the residents, "Your children play here. Don't make it a mosquito habitat. And why get in trouble with officials?"

The girls' posters and their extensive social service of cleaning up small infractions now and then kept them happy up there during their meetings. No night watchman was on patrol. They heard sounds coming from the faraway city and the train station. Far below, one bicycler rang his bell. They also heard the faint sounds of an auto rickshaw and car horns.

Ruma and Nalini knew they would not be disturbed where they were. They were brainstorming solutions to improve their morning commute to college. They were in their third year of undergraduate studies at an exclusive, women-only college. They sat on the concrete hugging their knees because Coimbatore was chilly in October.

"You're using big words, Ruma," Nalini said.

"Big words?" Ruma was edgy.

"You know, these are all nuisances if not inconveniences."

"I'm leaving!" Ruma was angry. She stood.

"Please don't be upset. Let's scrutinize this and find a solution today." Nalini pleaded.

"Okay, but let's not meander." Ruma sat.

This conversation took place in 1984 in Coimbatore, which is in southern India. It was a very industrialized city those days with several very well-known cotton mills including Lakshmi Mills. The nearby small town of Thiruppore exported men's underwear all over the world. Colleges were plentiful; most were en-route to the airport and cotton mills. There was a medical college known as CMC—Coimbatore Medical College. Famous PSG – (Peelamedu Samanaidu Govindarajanaidu) institutions ran colleges for arts, sciences, and engineering, and some were exclusively for girls. Many small-scale industries, mills, and offices were on the same route. Coimbatore was not called the Manchester of India for no reason.

The local government had not caught up with the immense if not sudden growth of the city. There was a dearth of not just water but just about everything else including transportation. Only three buses transported the masses to the colleges and workers to their mills and offices, and they were old and rickety. The morning commute could be an overwhelming experience and pretty much scary for the meek. Ruma and Nalini considered their commutes to be nightmares.

At the bus stop, Nalini, would stand and read a book oblivious to her surroundings and lost in the romantic Mills & Boon stories she read. Nalini was pretty by any standard. On the other hand, Ruma paid attention to everything around. She often looked at the entrance to the Selvasing Store, which had existed for over fifty years and sold just about everything under the sun. Since buses did not have proper schedules, college students congregated at the stop around eight as their classes started generally at eight forty-five.

The confreres dreaded boarding the bus. Ruma expressed her fear and anger while Nalini did not; she considered herself fearless. Buses were so packed that the locals would say, "If you dropped sesame seeds on top of this crowd, the seeds wouldn't reach the ground."

When the buses arrived, passengers would be hanging out the windows. Some would stand on one foot on the foot-board with the other foot hanging out. Once riders managed to get on the bus, they could barely move a limb. Considering the press, it was useless and laughable to spend time in the morning ironing clothes as they would be wrinkled quickly.

The metropolis was segregated into rich, poor, and middle-class sectors. The rich took their cars and motorcycles to school and work, the poor did not attend colleges but took buses to work, and the middle class could do neither. The overcrowded buses were somewhat filthy, but the auto rickshaws were unaffordable for them, especially for a daily commute.

It was not the overcrowding that burdened the savants; they could endure that for forty minutes. The problem was the aggressive, stealthy, and persistent touching, grabbing, groping, grinding, and sometimes even light kissing the girls were subjected to. Ruma called it molestation, but Nalini thought she was engaging in hyperbole.

"Nalini, this is *molestation*. It's not rape, but it's not just a nuisance, an annoyance, an inconvenience, or an indecency." She let that sink in. "This should be a criminal offense. This godforsaken country calls it simply Eve teasing. The idiots!"

Nalini saw that Ruma was enraged.

"One cannot manage it by just ignoring it or by thinking about quizzes or exams. No problem goes away by just disregarding it."

The guys who abused the girls did not bother the women who worked in the mills, or were vegetable peddlers, or office workers. But the young college women were easy targets. They looked classy and kept quiet on the bus except for wailing out occasionally that someone had stepped on their feet to get them to move away at least temporarily.

"Nellie, those who talk loudly on the bus or play lewd songs or whistle can be categorized as indecent as well." Ruma was angry. "Bus stops far from our apartments are a nuisance and an inconvenience too. So is someone taking seats reserved for the elderly and the handicapped. You can be fined for that kind of behavior."

Nalini tried to soothe Ruma. "It is indeed a civil offense."

"So why don't they fine people for groping us? Don't tell me it's just misbehaving because it definitely isn't!" Ruma was sharp, caustic.

"The conductor on the eight-a.m. bus is a good and conscientious fellow. When we don't have the exact fare and give him too much, he invariably gives us our change when we get off. Maybe we can secretly complain to him?" Nalini was in a solution mode.

"Public servants performing their duties without bribery? Indeed, what nobility! A laudable and noteworthy act! Good and conscientious fellows in a Gandhian nation!" A very dramatic Ruma resorted to mockery.

"Cynicism won't work."

"Sorry, Nellie, but it seems that someone did complain to him and he asked them to take an auto rickshaw to college if they wanted a clean ride. He sits at the back entrance and doesn't normally move around in the bus because there's absolutely no room for movement."

Auto rickshaws, cheaper versions of taxis, were too expensive for everyday commute, but Ruma's and Nellie's parents paid for them on the girls' exam days.

"Why don't we start taking our college bus again?"

Colleges, including theirs, had buses to take their students to and from school for a modest monthly fee.

"Been there done that, and we didn't like it a bit. Nell, do you remember why? They came at seven in the morning while our classes didn't start until eight forty-five. Almost two of our precious morning hours were wasted running around the city. We had to get up at five thirty to get ready for school and be at the stop by six forty-five just to drive all over the city to pick up other students—fifteen stops and about ten extra kilometers of riding the bus. I now know every nook and cranny of this damn city!"

"Yeah, and we couldn't attend evening classes or the drama and literary club, since college bus left exactly at 4 pm from the premises with students to be dropped off in the city". Nalini said.

The mention of the drama and literary club brought back a memory. "Remember our classmate-slash-actress?" Nalini mimed quotes and slashes with her fingers.

Lalitha was the classmate/actress Nalini was referring to. Lalitha wore precariously perched low-hip saris that Ruma and Nalini worried might drop off her hips if she walked faster. The girls had nick-named her LHL, meaning Low-Hip-Lalitta. She would get on the college bus and narrate at length the previous day's parties, movies she had seen, which cousin had flirted with whom, which uncle touched whom and where and at whose wedding all in an excited, shrill voice. There were always at least some ten girls around her. The entire bus would hear all about Lalitha's escapades.

"Okay, what would you call that kind of company on the bus?" Nalini asked; she was amused by Ruma's anger.

"Nonsense. That's what it is and what she is."

"You, literature students know apt words. Not bad, Ruma," Nalini said with a smile.

"If only she had boarded the bus near the end of our trip. Too bad her stop was right next to ours. Nellie, we're night owls. We couldn't get up that early. So, forget that. Let's think of ways to keep these guys on the bus away from us."

They didn't dare file a complaint with the police because some police officers were treacherous, and some police stations were infamous for torturing those they arrested who could not pay bribes. Distinguishing between the good, the bad, the ugly, and the callous policemen was a task the girls didn't want to undertake.

"It shouldn't be this difficult. If only the police system worked."

"Why don't I ask my dad to send a letter to the editor at the *Illustrated Weekly* or the *Indian Express* about our situation?"

"Sure, Nellie. That's a great idea. Ask him to write. Your father is a perfectionist. He sets high goals. It may take him several weeks to write this, and then they'll have to publish it, but it could be years before the government does anything about it. We may never see any change in our lives! We might achieve our goals if we're not atychiphobics."

"What's that?"

"Someone driven by an extreme fear of failure who sets unrealistically high goals to give him or her supposedly valid excuses for never achieving them."

They couldn't risk yelling at those who molested them on the bus because that could prompt the hooligans to follow them home when they got off. Showing resentment openly had repercussions. If the girls exposed this lawless behavior in public, the hooligans came to their backyards. They walked outside their home in the evenings or weekends. They didn't want to face retaliation, and they didn't want their younger sisters to be put in danger either.

"Wish we could take a ladies-only bus."

A college run by Christian nuns had fought for a ladies-only bus with the local government and was running it successfully to their college, which was on the other side of the city.

The girls were afraid that if they told their parents about the harassment they had to endure, that might result in their being transferred to some other college or having to take courses by correspondence which were notorious for subpar quality of education.

"Nellie, there's no point in longing for women-only buses or other solutions. Enough is enough. We women have had to adjust our lives everywhere and in every sphere. It's time for us to enjoy college before we graduate and become run-of-the-mill working women. Didn't Gandhi say, 'A man is but a product of his thoughts'? What we accomplish should change their thought processes. I cannot let them get off scot-free. Their charming selves are to be disgusted by us and keep themselves away from us deliberately just as we do."

Ruma planned to go to Madras, the city where she said life flourished, to get a master's degree in law, and Nalini wanted to be an actuary, the new and difficult subject slowly coming into in vogue in the insurance industry.

"Can we try the needle-pricking trick again?"

"No. That's difficult, and they could grab it and prick us back. It's easy to perceive who has it in her hand, and until it's used, it can just sting our own palms. It's been tried before by many but in vain. We can eliminate it without going the trial and error method."

"Have you noticed that they don't for some reason bother the women who work in the mills and the peddlers? Why are they spared and not us?"

"Don't know. They're all middle-aged men, probably married with children. "Don't know. They all look alike. Some are mill workers. Some are office goers. We don't know where the others work."

"You didn't answer my question. Do they spare their coworkers? Are they worried about the women complaining to their bosses at work? Or do they have general respect for coworkers?"

"Respect my foot! If women workers complained about a bus incident to their supervisors, the women would be the losers."

"Maybe we just smell better," Nalini said with a chuckle.

Ruma stared at Nalini. What looked like a bright halo shined around her face.

"Wow! Eureka! Nellie, you gave me the answer. You're a genius. You're not a math major for nothing. That's it!" Ruma was excited.

"What is it? Did my answer give a solution?"

"Yes, it did. I've thought of doing this before, but your answer has confirmed that it's actually *the* solution. Come here. I want to give you a hug! I'll whisper it."

Nalini drew near, and Ruma muttered her plan into her ear.

"My goodness!" Nalini burst into such laughter that she had to hold her stomach.

"Obscene behavior begets simple but nasty punishment." Ruma suddenly turned desperate. "It would make them run from us. The scent will make them associate college girls with it!"

"But how do we execute it?"

"I'll go to the doctor's dispensary tomorrow for a small empty bottle that contains medicine for an injection, an injection-bottle, one that has a rubber lid, from the garbage behind the building."

"Why that apparatus?"

"It will contain the odor until it's opened, which we can do easily with a nudge of a thumb. It's small, so we can hide it in our hands and open it in a few stops after we board the bus."

"Next question—why exactly feces? Why not a smelly chemical from our lab?"

"Many such compounds are toxic and can cause eye irritation, nausea, and headaches. And it's not easy to lift anything from our labs."

"How about a rotten fish?"

"That would require a big one. And why waste products we'd have to buy? Bodily defecation is the only suitable answer."

"Okay, so we don't leave any stones unturned, We'll have to wear gloves while picking them up.."

"I know the drill, Nalini. I've run this scene many times in my mind. These items are aplenty. I don't have to touch more than one. I could even ask the compounder in the dispensary to give me some empty unused bottles. I can tell him I'm building a model car with them. These are small but sturdy. They won't break by dropping. In that crowd, they might not even fall to the floor."

Ruma had indeed gone through this several times in her mind, but Nalini wasn't completely convinced.

"We're going with the theory that the lingering awful smell will drive them nuts. But in actuality, many things could happen. I'll be the devil's advocate here. Let's run all the possibilities in our minds. Scenario one: the bottle is found at his feet. Of course, no one would want to touch it. But someone notices it and throws up. People look for a suspect. Someone gives the news to the local newspapers. Some of them run stories like this, and the trashy ones will run them for sure. If our compounder at the dispensary reads them, he may remember us and connect it. Didn't you say Dr. Raghu owns the dispensary and he's your family doctor? He might let him know."

"Okay, let's not get it from the compounder. Let's swipe it from the dispensary garbage at night. Let's walk by the dispensary to see if there are any streetlights above the garbage."

"Scenario number two: Could someone identify the dispensary by the type of vial we use?"

"Nope. They're all the same type, so no one could identify any one dispensary that way. Don't think they would go to such lengths. No sleuths diligent enough in Coimbatore."

"We haven't read hundreds of Sherlock Holmes stories for nothing."

"Hmm, Nellie, I'm still a bit jittery about this. The garbage may have used sponges and exposed blood. Can't we come up with a different container? Maybe a perfume bottle?"

"None that small."

"An empty match Box?"

"That wouldn't contain the smell, and it could get soggy."

"A small tin container?"

"No, the lid cannot be opened inconspicuously or even easily in a crowded bus."

They considered and rejected other containers as too big or not easy enough to open. They needed a reliable biohazard urn.

"Let's go scavenger hunting on Friday afternoon at the mills."

But the mills were surrounded by tall concrete walls with broken glass pieces set into mortar atop and guarded at the entrances.

"Let's ditch the idea about the Coimbatore mills."

"How about a Thiruppore mill?"

Thiruppore was the mecca of cotton mills. Due to their sheer number, they thought they could find something there surely at least in an alley. It was an hour away by train. Trains were somewhat the opposites of buses—there wasn't a problem getting a seat on them.

"We could take the train from Coimbatore Junction, walk the streets of Thiruppore until we find something suitable, and catch the train back in the afternoon. We could walk home from the station. It's only about a mile from here."

"Hope no one we know travels on those trains."

"Yes, that's always the risk. Our parents can never learn about this. That would spell the end of our college studies."

"We should leave a little late, after the morning crowd. Maybe take the ten o'clock train, which will get us there around eleven, too late for the morning crowd to reach there. There are no stops between the North Coimbatore Station and Thiruppore. We should scan the station before boarding. We see one familiar face, we go home."

"We can tell our parents we have no classes that morning and are taking a later bus. By the time we leave for the station, they would've gone to work, and we'd get back before them as usual."

"College will want a letter from our parents explaining our absence."

"Get a forged one ready. We've been there and done that."

The perplexed girls had a penchant for Bollywood Hindi movies, which were shown in just one theatre during the mornings. They never missed one. They were crazy for Hindi film music, for R. D. Burman, the music director who sent them spinning to an entirely different planet, and for the voices of Mukesh, Kishore Kumar, and Latha Mangheskar, which left them weeping. Not knowing a word of Hindi was an added advantage, a supportive inconvenience they thought; they could imagine the dialogue and the lyrics themselves. The two had had seen a few morning screenings and had no problems forging their parents' signatures on the letters they took to college the next day— "Due to sickness, my daughter was unable to attend classes yesterday. Signed————"

"Okay, let's reconvene right here Friday night after our Thiruppore sojourn."

They took the ladder down and walked to their homes past the cricket pitch.

The following Friday, the harassed girls walked to North Coimbatore Station and watched out for familiar faces. They were relieved to see none. They bought round-trip tickets and sat next to each other in the train eating their jelly-drenched sandwiches and taking the scenery in. The train's resident beggars, a young boy of about seven who was blind showing an unnatural alabaster white pupil led by a slightly older girl in a cottony, flowery, dirty, full skirt and an oversized red, buttoned-down men's shirt, serenaded the famous hilltop god of Marudamalai Murugan on the Western Ghats, which were part of Coimbatore. They wailed the god's name creating pathos.

> This concept of God
> May just be facade imagination, not ever existing
> A stone-statue product from a chisel of an architect
> But
> The wondrous light that you are, Ocean of compassion
> In Your luminous luster, my heart will never ever be
> lost
> will always laud.

Someone in first class must have asked the lad to sing a movie song. The girls heard him sing a number by the great playback song writer Kannadasan, the ageless lyricist of the silver screen of the south. The warm poet's immortal verses turned placid and sometimes amorous with boundless and endless enthusiasm for life.

> The intelligent aren't always successful;
> The succeeded, not necessarily intelligent.
> The benevolent aren't big-moneyed;

The big-moneyed, not always benevolent.
The daydreamer, perfect in dreams
Fancies her in his dreams
In her's though, him, absent
Another man frequenting hers.
Not everyone falls in love
Not every love ends in marriage
Not every marriage ends in success
Not every success offers togetherness

The two teenagers gave the boy a rupee each. The girls saw that some give them snacks, sandwiches, and packets of peanuts. Ruma pledged to give a better life to young boys and girls when she became a lawyer in three years. Ruma and Nellie agreed to give another rupee—fifty paisa each—to an elderly beggar though the distressed neophytes agreed that they weren't sure if he would buy food or alcohol. "It's his karma, not ours, if he abuses his alms," they concluded.

The majestic Malabar Mountains bordering the city on the west permitted just about enough rain for the coconut and plantain groves of Coimbatore. The British called them the Blue Mountains while the locals called them the Neelgiris, Neel meaning blue and Giris meaning mountains. The British had had their secluded golf links and country clubs, posh boathouses, and botanical gardens in Ooty, a hill station in the Neelgiris. Adjacent to Ooty was Coonoor, which housed the Pasteur Institute and its museum. Budding scientists thronged the institute those days, and everyone was likely to land in Coimbatore or Bangalore, later called the Tech City, to get to Coonoor or Ooty. They were swell tourist spots, great reprieves from the scorching sun with the famous Doddabetta Peak, tea factories where tea tasting conjured many, horse-riding, and Hindustan Photo Films, which developed India's movie films and employed many. The Mudumali Wildlife Sanctuary attracted photographers from *National Geographic*, naturalists from every corner of the world, and tourists.

When Ruma and Nellie got off at Thiruppore Station, hot air blew in their faces. The almost empty narrow roads compacting heat welcomed them brimming with promises. The two girls were on a mission impossible; they walked silently as they closely inspected the streets and the alleys but saw nothing that would suit their purposes. They thought of the Noyyal River and walked there, but they did not find anything useful except for a few pieces of cloth that were stamped with the name of the manufacturer, which they took. They went back to the train station tired and exhausted from roaming the streets in the very hot weather. They boarded the two o'clock train back to Coimbatore and happily did not see anyone they recognized.

When the two girls met on the concrete underneath the water tank that night, the plan was finalized. They found an injection device outside the dispensary after dark the following day and lined it with some of the cloth with the mill logo on it facing out. They put a rubber lid on top of the carafe and the cloth. When Ruma or

Nalini flipped it open, they engaged it enough to make sure the cloth did not come out. The &%#@^itself was to be placed on the bottom and sides of the reliquary as well as the cloth so that the cloth would stick to the capsule. The cloth was to there to connect the culprit to the mills or just as a diversion for any type of investigation.

They did without gloves to forgo the expense and because it was a small town when it came to someone buying gloves. They wrapped their hands with plastic grocery bags and secured them with rubber bands.

Their determination glowed from their faces. "We are the big baller brand to pull this trigger. But one little detail—what if our saris and skirts get tainted from an awkward drop? We certainly can't walk around smelling like #^%#&%% the entire day at college. When we go for drama club practice on Sunday, let's take a change of clothes and store them in our desks."

"Great thinking," Ruma said nodding happily.

"If the package rolls after being dropped, and if it doesn't get dragged outside by any passenger, it will remain in the bus to be found by the janitors cleaning the bus that night."

"I'm sure they'll just sweep it out along with all sorts of junk. No one will examine it."

"If the conductor examines the bus after eleven when it gets back to the bus station, he may question it, but no one will have the patience to examine it after a long day. We're covered even if someone ponders."

"Our plan is elaborate but well thought-out to keep them away and not get caught."

"Why did Thiruppore mills have a Coimbatore mill logo?"

"Maybe a collaboration. Don't know. I've seen that logo on clothes from our Coimbatore mills. Irrelevant to us but helpful."

Ruma comforted her friend before getting off the slab. "Nalini, don't you worry. This is a small punishment for a big crime. All I want is for them to stay away from us."

"Are we going to repeat this?"

"Only if necessary. It may not work if we repeat it too often. Maybe on different buses. If this doesn't work, we'll have to innovate to keep them away and it's more important to teach them a lesson. We'll get our degrees and pursue careers without their actions disturbing our thoughts, but their acts shouldn't go unpunished. What about our sisters and other girls who will ride the buses for years?"

"A barrister on the rise. A bar-at-law could devise a permanent solution, right?"

"That may take me a while, Nellie. I want revenge right now. India could be an ancient country but it's a young nation, independent only for thirty-seven years. This is a very short period for a nation to see a lot of growth but at the same time, with a lot of potential to grow"

"What made you think of executing this idea above all other ones?"

"What other ideas? We didn't have any others that were workable.

I noticed they didn't trouble the other ladies on the bus much. They don't bother that woman who wears the forest-green mill uniform, the one who's on the bus when we board it. She's cute and young and looks like a factory worker. They don't bother that peddler woman with a vegetable basket. It's always just us, the college girls. We may not know who those thugs are – but looks like they don't want to harass someone who could get them in trouble at work. We must look easy, or maybe we smell better. When you jokingly said we may be the chosen ones for that reason, my heart flipped. Just getting something repulsive may just do the trick. Worth trying and proving to ourselves if our theory is right."

"Risky, though. What if someone saw us drop the vials?"

"In that crowd? No way. Also, we don't drop it right away. Wait for a stop or two, let more people in."

"How many receptacles are we going to fill up?"

"Whatever can be discerned quickly, in a short sweep, and without a lot of problems."

"Umm, one small detail. Are you regular every morning?"

"A cup of hot coffee might just do it."

"Just let me know after your morning ablutions."

"Ablutions? Really? Look who's chastising me for my words!"

"Just got carried away. Math majors know a word or two too you know."

They laughed until their sides ached.

"Why do you think I told you my plan?" Ruma said. "You're my backup."

"We can even get some to rub off on him if we're lucky. That would be even better."

"@#%^ for a @#%^ty man!"

"What do we do after the smell spreads?"

"Lasso His Cheapness with our harrowing smell of a noose," she said feigning spinning a long Western lasso, holding a coil of it in her left hand.

Nellie clapped and tipping her imaginary cowboy hat to Ruma. The pair endlessly admired Clint Eastwood in *The Good, the Bad, and the Ugly* having traveled as far as Madras, eight hours by train, to see the film with other fans.

"We act shocked and appalled just as anyone else in the bus would be. That will convey the message that it wasn't us. We should rehearse it on Sunday," Nellie said.

Ruma said, "Hey, as long the mood is busted, it'll be good enough. It may change his perception in a bad way of course, but it'll serve him right. They say smell and taste are a lot more complicated than people think. To most people, a smell isn't just a fragrance—it's also a memory. It may leave an indelible impression on his brain that he associates with college girls."

"Pretty Priya may puke from the odor. She's done that before. But that's fine—the more commotion the better."

Priya was also a regular in their bus; she attended the same college.

"We know we'll never get seats on that bus, and the ride is always uncomfortable, but we just can't accept that behavior ever. We're not throwing &^&^*& on them just to squelch our anger. We're doing this for our sisters and their generation too."

"Yes, we women scorned should first believe and understand that there *is* such a thing as Personal space even on public transportation because we are paying for our rides. Despite your disagreement with my choice of word for this act, which is by the way the appropriate and correct one, don't we agree that at least a line must be drawn that will enable everyone to be peaceful before they get to their destinations? We shouldn't be attending our morning classes with spiked blood pressure every day and dread the evening commute either."

"Okay, and after we accomplish this, our next mission is to get rid of the roadside Romeos perched on the compound walls singing lewd songs looking at girls or following them. We shouldn't be looking for a company every day to walk with us all the time."

"Yes, those balls on walls? At least they don't touch us. They're just doing it movie style. Hero walks behind a college heroine and sings suggestive songs. She shows her back to the hero but smiles and enjoys the whole ordeal to the camera."

"Can't we write to some movie directors saying we really don't enjoy that charade?"

"Ha! Funny."

"We could take out slippers from our feet and show it to them as girls do on the street or sing something louder than they are."

"Nellie, you're a genius! You're not a math major for nothing. Let's be louder than them on the street and drown out their lyrics."

"How? Sing a song in reply? That would be hideous not to mention encouraging."

"No, not a song. Do you know any Sanskrit mantra or a regular, everyday *shloka*?"

"Just the one on Ganesa, our elephant God—four short lines. My mother makes me say it every evening when she lights the lamp at the altar."

"That's the only one I know as well. Let's say it aloud as we walk, and the boys are following us. We'll recite the lines and repeat them if they whistle or vomit suggestiveness until they shut their foul mouths."

"Should try it. It'll be ridiculous in the middle of the street."

"So be it. Simple solutions for everyday problems."

"Why not? But first things first. Let's see if we are successful in throwing %$^$ on them on the bus and then deal with the Don Juans, the Casanovas."

The two friends laughed and talked for another hour excited about their Monday-morning commute and eager for results.

"We'll create havoc. Let the intoxication greet our bus on Monday."

"That's wicked. The douchebag's tension will be a scene. Let's shake the combat from its half slumber." A gleeful Nellie stretched out.

After Nellie dozed off that night, she dreamed that the hoodlum on the bus was chasing her with a large machete, very popular in the villages around Coimbatore due to their heavy usage in communal and family fights for properties and so-called honor killings. She woke up drenched in sweat and with a pounding heart, but she did not let that deter her.

True to their word, on that Saturday night, the scholars worked quietly, efficiently, and diligently. After dinner, they walked daringly to Gandhi Puram, a dispensary on Seventh Street. Peering cautiously when entering the street, the penny-pinching tightwads tightened the makeshift gloves on their left hands. They quickly swept the top of the garbage and found some vials. It was flawless. They went back and washed them with a phenol solution and soap in Nalini's bathroom.

As Monday dawned, the conspirators met at the bus stop well before eight with shiny, obscure, cloth-lined, rubber-lidded vials of #$@#$@ in their hands. They wanted to change the ambiance, the vibrations—their halos and their karma.

STORY 3

No Escape

How poor are they that have not Patience!
What wound did ever heal but by degrees?

—William Shakespeare (1564–1616)

In 1984, the twins immigrated to the United States from India and became undergraduate students at Ohio State. The sisters were about eighteen when they were added as minors on the I-130 form that their good physician brother had used to sponsor his lonely mother for a green card.

The twins were barely out of middle school and were about thirteen when their father passed away. Their older brother was completing his medical degree though he was only twenty-two. In India, students could enter medical school right out of high school, but it was one of the most coveted and toughest college admissions to capture in the nation. There weren't many private institutions, and many government-run medical college admissions were rife with corruption.

Dr. Veera had come to the United States in 1980. He was going to be a family practitioner. His residency was in the University Hospitals in Columbus, Ohio, and he took a job there after his residency. He liked the small-town feel of Columbus, and he had made many friends from India as well there.

What he could not digest was that Columbus had not one south Indian restaurant then. If he and his friends felt like *dosa*, they had to drive to Cincinnati. There was an Indian restaurant in Columbus at the corner of Lane Avenue and High Street, but it catered only to north Indian palates. His weekend trips to Cincinnati when he was not on call had become a routine.

His mother asked him to get married, but he vehemently refused. "My wedding bells will ring only after the twins are settled down, Mom."

"But they're nine years younger than you. They'll settle down in due time. Don't you worry about them please."

She couldn't bear the thought of her hard-working son not eating properly; she feared that he would start eating meat, a thought that tormented her constantly.

"Mom, there's plenty of vegetarian choices available here. I eat a healthy salad, and I can now cook our sambar, curries, and whatnot. Your daughter-in-law will be a lucky girl." Dr. Veera chuckled.

"She will indeed be a lucky woman, Veera! To marry someone like you, she would have done a lot of good Karma."

Veera's mother was very proud of her intelligent and honest son. He was responsible beyond what she had ever hoped for. He promised to sponsor her and the twins as soon as he became a citizen of the United States. He would educate his siblings in the States and would fuss until the twins were settled in good jobs before he married.

"Indeed, I am lucky, and the twins are very blessed."

"My son got in without our paying a penny to any government officials" was a prideful point Veera's mother loved to make. Getting a green card for a widowed mother was not a problem in 1984. They waited for about eighteen months and were there in the United States.

He brought them to his spacious, four-bedroom home off Bethel Road in Columbus close to his practice. The twins had rooms of their own, their mother had another, and the bathroom was clean with no dampness on the floor. They could drink water right from the tap anytime they wanted, and they did not see any cockroaches. They were on cloud nine!

The twins, Rohini (Rohin to her mother and Veera) and Revathi (Reva to her mother and Rey to Veera) started undergraduate studies in September 1984. Since Veera needed the only car they had, the twins took public transportation; the buses were heated in the winter and cooled in the summer, and they were not crowded at all. That was unheard of in India, they cheerfully noted.

They could read until their stop was coming up. They would just press the yellow strip near every seat before their stop and the driver would pull over and let them off. The driver greeted them when they boarded the bus and wished them "Good day," or "Have peachy Monday," or something they had never heard before and lively wishes when they got off. They would chime back to him as they had come to enjoy the rides immensely.

Foreordained to take the same classes for the first two years, they went to the café in the union in the afternoons and supplemented their *rotis*, which they would eat with ketchup, mustard, or relish and have salads or a slice of pizza they would cut lengthwise, so each got some crust.

Many Indian students there had been born and brought up in the United States and looked and carried themselves differently from them. "They're Americans just born of Indian parents. We're still Indians. Maybe in another five or ten years, we'll be like them," Rohini said; she was the more optimistic of the two. Rohini was incredibly alive sometimes painfully so.

"No, Rohin. We're just not cool. That's all the reason we stand separate though the generic similarity is Indian ancestry. We're busy studying all the time. We can't stand it when we miss one point on a test, and we argue endlessly with our teachers in our accents for that one point. We also compare our papers with others and see who did better. We worry and obsess over our grades. Most important, though, we still wear our long Indian *kurta* over our jeans and shawls to cover our torsos. Do you see where we are different? Last but not least, we don't date or drink," said Revathi, the more perceptive one.

After their sophomore year, Rohini decided to major in journalism and Revathi studied for a degree in mechanical engineering. Rohini's classes were in the College of Arts and Science and Revathi's in the School of Engineering.

The two started leaving home at different times and coming back late; Rohini worked with the school paper *Lantern*, and Revathi spent hours in the lab. There were no buses at that late hour, and with their brother's weird hours, they couldn't depend on him to pick them up. Veera suggested that the girls should live on campus to solve the problem, and so they got dorm rooms.

The brother and sisters hardly ever saw each other then without planning. Rohini took a trip to India to meet a few prospective husbands; Their mother said 'boys' lined-up to marry Rohini due to her green-card status.

Revathi said no to that and stayed behind. The lucky sisters were in great demand since their green cards meant future citizenship for them, and that would change the fortunes of well-educated boys in India who dreamed of getting to the States.

Rohini wanted the best of the best—a medical doctor or someone with an engineering degree from IIT; She will marry the one with the greatest potential to make the most money. Rohini was in great demand. Rohini said she was going to stay home and be a writer and the ideal situation for her is to land a good and wealthy man and that she had worked hard to make ends meet for the past several years! Not anymore, she confirmed.

Rohini got engaged; the marriage would take place after she completed her undergraduate studies and became a citizen.

During her India trip, they registered their nuptials like a civil wedding in a municipal registrar's office in the presence of their mothers and close relatives for witnesses so Rohini could come back to the States and start the paperwork for her husband-to-be to join her.

Rey, as Revathi called herself after becoming a citizen, expressed her desire to fall in love before marrying. "An engrossing chemistry is an absolute necessity for me."

That caused Rohini to rationalize the matter. "Arranged marriages are like new jobs. You network, you prepare a resume, and you apply for available jobs that suit your interest after studying the company background. The prerequisites are the same—a college degree, decent credentials, and skills. You interview and accept an offer or not. You ask friends and family about the firm that offered you the job. You do all due diligence, and then you leap in excitement. You try to do a good job, but you do make mistakes. You learn to create a chemistry with coworkers and their families. You love it or despise it. You keep it or quit and look for a new job."

"That's the most awful comparison I've ever heard," Rey said. "Where's love and chemistry, in this"?

"Chemistry should happen during the first meeting. If it does not, you do not pursue that alliance".

Rey let it go as she was not interested in hurting Rohini.

Rohini resumed her studies after returning from India; she spoke weekly with her husband-on-paper. She called it her courtship period.

The twins showed up at Veera's home on some Friday or Saturday nights and watched scary movies or Bollywood romances they rented from a nearby Blockbuster. Rohini may have had something to do with that; she had acquired the names and addresses of some Blockbuster bigwigs and had repeatedly written to them about offering Bombay movies. At home, Rohini would tape them as she watched them, and she created a small library that she and her mother watched repeatedly. Rohini was more fluent in Hindi than Rey and Veera were.

They all had friends including some they had known in India who came to the US after finishing undergrad studies there and wanted to reconnect with the twins. Their home off Bethel Road was abuzz with activity—someone would show up for a home-cooked meal, or Indian students at OSU would be invited over by their mother for *dosas*. A keyboard player and his band showed up from Madurai to practice in their basement for Independence Day, August 15. Students living in dorms or apartments loved coming to the spacious house for lunches, dinners, and tea.

Rey had signed up for a summer class, but Rohini wanted the summer off. That Saturday afternoon, Rey was dozing on the couch. Her late-night movie habit and her newly formed habit of drinking and getting hangovers kept her on the couch. Rohini, who had slept until noon, was reading in the living room.

The house had a staircase to the right as one stood at the entrance and a living room to the left. Veera had made it cozy and warm with tapestries from India on the one wall facing the door and an ornate and beautiful red rug on top of the boring beige carpet all over the house. If one entered from the front door, continued to walk straight on the long foyer, past the living room, which was on the left to the foyer, one ended up in their kitchen. On to the right side of the Kitchen was the vast breakfast area. If one crossed the breakfast area they could reach the family room with the French doors leading to the backyard. On the other side of the Kitchen was the dining room, which was adjacent to the front living room. A short hallway from the breakfast area led to the garage. The security system chimed every time someone opened a door or a window on the first floor.

The doorbell rang, and Rohini answered it. "Hi, Suresh. Come on in." Rohini sounded as if she had been expecting him. Rey's doubts about that were clarified when she heard Rohini say, "Finally you're here. How long did it take you?"

"About three and a half hours."

Why does he sound familiar? Rey asked herself.

"Mom's upstairs taking an afternoon siesta, and Veera is in the hospital doing rounds."

"I can wait until Veera comes, that is, if he comes before eight. Rohin, tell me, how are you? How's United States treating you?"

Rey heard a pleasant happiness in his voice.

"Oh, we're fantastic. I'll be finishing my BA soon, and Rey will complete her degree as well. Can I get you some chai?"

"Oh, I won't leave without eating your mom's home-cooked dinner, so don't you worry."

Suresh examined the living room. "Rohini, who decorated this room? It's exquisite!"

"Definitely not me," Rohini said laughing. "If you're waiting to know if it was my engineer sister, nope, she didn't either. Veera had an interior decorator do the whole thing."

It finally dawned on Rey that Suresh was the older brother of one of Rohini's high school classmates. Though the twins had attended the same high school, Rey had shifted to a nearby college for the last two years of her high school since the math classes she was eligible to take were not available at their high school. Rey had seen Suresh's sister around but had not known her well enough to remember her name. Rohini had many friends, and Rey was simply not up to getting to know them all. She often left home if Rohini invited her friends over for lunch or for a study group.

"By the way, let me see if my sis is around."

Rohini left the living room, and Rey heard her steps approaching her.

Rohini stood for a few seconds wondering if she should wake Rey up. She went back to the living room and announced, "She's asleep,

Suresh. We watched a late-night movie. Rey actually got up early but must have gone back to take a nap or something. Should be up soon."

"Don't wake her up. I can wait."

"I know you would after having come all the way from Pittsburgh to see her."

A sudden sharp heartburn hit Rey's chest; she curled up due to what felt like a stab. She was fully awake at that point and keenly listening to the conversation.

"Rohini, didn't you tell Rey I was coming to see her as well?"

"Are you kidding? She's a demon when it comes to me or anyone else arranging suitors for her. She wouldn't have come home at all this Saturday if I'd opened my mouth about your visit."

"But I told you I'd come only if she wanted to meet me."

"Oh, it'll be fine. She can come and talk with you after she wakes up. There's absolutely no contract here, is there?"

Suresh changed the topic to the movie they had watched the previous night, some recent Indian hits, his accomplishments at Carnegie Mellon—the topics moved on. In between their conversation, Rohini came around a few times to check on Rey but did not wake her up. She went back to the living room with either some chai or Pakoras.

Rey's mind raced; she wanted to get out of the house without Rohini and Suresh knowing that, but she knew the security system would make its noise when she opened any door. *Maybe I can detach* the security wires on the laundry room window and get out that way. The laundry room was situated near the doors leading to the garage. But she remembered that Veera had told them that the alarm would sound if the wires were detached from the inside.

She felt trapped. *How dare my sister invite her friend's brother without my permission even when he had explicitly wanted her to fill me in ahead of time? What an insult! Who does she think she is? Does Veera know about this? How about Mom? What in the world?*

Rey's angry thoughts were interrupted when she heard the garage door open. She heard Rohini exclaim, "Veera's home!"

Rey's mathematical brain came up with an idea—wait until Veera opened the car door in the garage, open the door leading to the garage to make it sound as if Veera were coming in, stop Veera in the garage, and urge him to drive her to a donut shop on Henderson and Dierker Roads. When she heard Veera open the car door, she dashed to the door leading to the garage, opened and closed it behind her, and asked Veera to be quiet and get back in the car.

Once Veera got behind the wheel, she said, "Veera, please drive me to Henderson Road right away. I'll explain everything while you drive."

Veera drove silently without being perturbed; he had the calmness that comes with seeing patients in the emergency room; he just listened to Rey and dropped her off at the donut shop.

When he got back and came inside, Suresh rose and shook his

hand. Veera sat on the couch and exchanged pleasantries for a while; he excused himself to go upstairs and freshen up.

Rohini went into the family room to wake Rey up but did not find her there on the couch. She checked the half-bath near the laundry room but didn't see her there either.

As Veera was climbing the stairs, Rohini sprinted to the bottom of the stairs and looked up at Veera. "Did you see Rey on the couch?"

"Nope, I didn't."

"Where is she?" she muttered to herself. She told Suresh, "My sister was sleeping on the couch, but she's not there. Just a minute. Maybe she went to the fridge in the garage for something."

Rohini rushed to the garage, found no sign of Rey, and went back to the living room.

By then, their mother had come downstairs and was conversing with Suresh and asking about his family.

"Mom, did you see Rey upstairs?"

Without waiting for a reply, she climbed the staircase in four steps and ran into Rey's room. Finding it empty, she was puzzled. She ran to the basement thinking Rey was ironing laundry. Nope.

Suresh felt weird. He was puzzled as to where Rey was too. Veera kept telling them that Rey must have taken the bus back to school without knowing about Suresh's visit. He said Rey would call from the dorm to announce her safe arrival there, a routine they had established.

When a call came later in the evening, Veera confirmed that Rey had called to assure them that she had reached her room.

Suresh had an early dinner and left around seven. Veera insisted that he take a coffee to go since his mom made the best filtered coffee. Veera was also worried that Suresh might stop at the conspicuous donut shop where he had dropped Rey off; she was there waiting for Veera to pick her up.

After Suresh's departure, Veera went back to the donut shop. Rey jumped in his car with a box of munchkins. Brother in a plush work outfit and sister in poor sartorial sleep-ins got home quickly.

Rohini's confusion was written all over her face when she saw Rey. "What the heck? Why? Where were you? I thought you went back to the dorm."

"How dare you invite a guy to meet me without telling me a word about it?"

"Who said I asked Suresh to come see you? He wanted to come to see all of us."

"Liar! I heard you discuss it explicitly."

"Skye bitch! I never did!"

Rohini had by then learned all the curse words and had no qualms about using them.

Veera's face turned red. "C'mon, stop it. To the family room right now, both of you. Sit right there and listen to me without another word. I'm going to humor myself by instilling some sense into you pachyderms. I talked with Suresh and learned he had come here on Rohini's invitation, and I also know that you, Rohini, didn't tell any of us about his coming here today from Carnegie Mellon. Now you better have some good explanation for inviting him and not apprising us of that."

"Well, why should I alert any of you? He said he wanted to come, and I said fine."

"Okay then, so why were you pouncing on Rey because she snuck out?"

"He wanted to see her, and he waited a long time for her to wake up. So, I was upset."

"Rohini, do you realize that you could have easily woken her up had Rey really been asleep and that she was just pretending to be asleep? Why didn't you figure out Rey didn't want to see him?"

"Again, Veera, I didn't invite him to fix them up or anything."

Rohini was in tears; the others knew she would start crying in an attempt to elicit Veera's and Rey's sympathy. Rohini could cry at the drop of a hat and make an innocent bystander a criminal.

"Your crying won't deter me today, Rohini," Veera said.

"Veera, you said it!" Rey said. "I've dreaded her crying all my life. You've noticed it too?" She turned to Rohini. "Here—yoohoo! *I'm* the victim here. Shouldn't I be the one crying? Just how *do* you do that—cry at your whim?"

Veera pretended to ignore Rey. "Rohin, you invited him, he came, and that's that. If he wanted to meet Rey, he should have contacted her through you or us. Isn't that the transparent way of doing this?"

"What would have been wrong about her getting up and saying hi to him? That doesn't require much."

"What's *wrong?*" Rey asked rhetorically. "Where can I begin? How about educating me about his interest in meeting me? How about my interest in this at all? How about owning your mistake at least once without hiding in your tears? How about honesty? Surely you could give that a try once in a while." Tyrannical sarcasm was her forte.

Rohini wasn't a straight-faced liar. It came out immediately since the fight progressed without any end in sight. "Okay, let me be honest. I asked Suresh to come to help Veera." She was waiting for her brother's praise.

"To help me?" Veera's surprise and a good-natured chuckle encouraged Rohini.

"Yes! Now that I'm engaged, I thought it would be helpful for you if Rey started meeting men. You could finally settle down once we were both married. Suresh had been asking me to meet with Rey, so I asked him to come. I knew this devil would have jumped up and down if I told her, so I just asked Suresh to make it to Columbus without your knowledge. I didn't want either one of us to be a stumbling block for Veera's happiness."

Put Veera in the equation, Rey will calm down, she thought.

Veera's words reflected his irritation at that. "Oh oh oh! STOP! Let me make this clear. Neither of you is hindering my way to happiness or whatever nonsense you're carping about. Rohin, just listen and listen well. Just as you decided to marry on your own terms, Rey will one day get married on her own terms. Don't try rushing anyone into anything. period. I'm not waiting for either of you for anything, and I never thought you two were my job or duty to complete." He chuckled. "I'll settle down when I'm ready. Promise me not to get your nose into anybody's business from now on."

"Thank you, Veera," Rey said. "I really appreciate that."

That was the first time Veera had taken sides, but he had learned to be calm.

Rohini was still sobbing but was quieting down on the couch. However, she was not apologizing.

"Why the hell are you standing in front of me?" Rohini yelled at Rey, who had gone over to the couch and was standing in front of her with her hands on her hips.

"You owe me an apology," Rey pronounced as she glared intensely at Rohini ignoring Veera and their mother. "In fact, she owes one to Mom and Veera as well."

"Apology my foot! You're the one who owes me an apology. If you hadn't pretended to be asleep and had come in to just say hi to Suresh, all this could have been averted!"

"You're incorrigible," Rey yelled and ran upstairs knowing there would be no apology from Rohini; her mother wouldn't demand that of Rohini, and Veera would have just kept quiet as usual.

Rey stayed upstairs; she heard her mother lamenting, "I thought they would be congenial to each other being twins and all. It's my bad karma that they don't behave even like regular sisters."

About an hour later, Veera called from downstairs, "Rey, want to go with me and Rohin to Blockbuster for a movie?"

Rey would have pretended not to have heard him, but hey, he was Veera. She ran to the landing and saw Veera standing on the first step. "Nope, not going. Have work."

"You sure? Do you have any choices? Would you watch a movie at all?"

"Nope. I have schoolwork to complete."

He left with a simple "Okay."

From her window, Rey saw his Camry leave and saw it come back twenty minutes later.

The threesome watched something Rey heard the credit song for, but she wasn't interested. She thought, *whatever happened to something called an apology? Mom doesn't care about it or know one even exists, but Veera knows the etiquette, but even he didn't ask Rohini to apologize.*

Bollywood movies had popular numbers, and Rey would watch one if she could sing some of them. Otherwise, Hindi, though the national language of India, eluded her. The Dravidian movements had banned the southerners from learning Hindi, keeping their state, Tamil Nadu, the only state not to know the national language. Tamils, who were captivated to work in other parts of India, sought English as the means of communication in which they excelled or spoke broken Hindi and became the laughingstock of the rest of the country. The Hindi-speaking students who had come from India, just like the twins, at OSU didn't care much for her or Rohini in their gatherings since they did not understand the jokes or knew any Hindi movies.

Rey heard Veera come up about half an hour into the movie and shut his room door. Veera's movie watching was a joke. He either slept half the time or left and came upstairs ten or twenty minutes into the movie. He went to theaters to watch mainstream movies, and she hoped he watched them to the end. *It was sweet that he thought of renting a movie to ease the tension at home*, Rey thought. But the ones who usually bent over backward to watch Indian movies at home were usually Rohini and their mother.

Around midnight when Rey got up to use the restroom, she overheard her mother telling Rohini how hard it would be for Veera to get two girls settled down and that they should not make it any more difficult for him than it already was and so on. She knew that Veera and her mother were on her side.

After that incident, Rohini tried to pacify Veera. She wrote a short poem for him:

"To be a first-born, over a pair of quibbling twins
Oh, what overwhelming idiotic Shenanigans
You must have overcome all with your fortitude
Showed us the way in your endearing attitude.

Respect for women in your life unparalleled
Love within your heart naturally channeled
Towards everyone, enabling us to herald
Into your sweet home, we journaled.

In this marvelous journey of life in bliss
What a blessing to be able to reminisce
To hold, cherish, love for ever to peace
Dr. Veera, my brother has earned his glories

To have Mom and you, I feel accomplished
You both made sure I am well established
Your patience and ease of heart distinguished
Let my love for you every day be replenished"

Dr. Veera read her poem, smiled and asked her to continue to write and left it at that!

The twins' division grew wider, after Suresh's incident and it didn't seem that it would be repaired anytime soon. Rey was careful not to visit home when Rohini was around.

If you are facing Dr. Veera's domicile, you see that to the right is an alley between his house and his neighbors that ran to their backyards. The window in Veera's laundry room looked out on the alley. In the 80s it was not common for homeowners to mount cameras to protect their homes. Veera and others in the basement had noticed passers-by in the alley and that was disconcerting to say the least.

Once, Rohini walked down the alley to the patio; she wanted to wash off some mud stuck to her shoe. On the way, she found a bunch of quarters, dimes, and nickels. She excitedly rounded them up and counted them—about three dollars. She ran to the patio. "Veera, Rey, Mom! Look what I found in the alley!"

The three of them had just entered the home from the garage; they ran to the patio door and opened it for the hollering girl, who said, "Found all this in our alley!" Rohini showed them the coins.

"Wow! How much?" Veera and Rey asked in chorus.

"About three dollars!" Rohini was beaming. "I'm getting a Friendly's peanut-buster parfait."

But she saved the money, and she continued finding more coins in the alley every once in a while. By the end of the year, she had found about eleven dollars in coins. She treated it like a lottery win. Veera made fun of her, and Rey found it to be mystery since she herself had never found a penny out there.

Veera tried to rationalize the matter. "People walk through the alley as a shortcut from Dierker and Bethel Roads to the cul-de-sac. They perhaps dropped the coins as they fished in their pockets for a cigarette lighter. The alley is just mud and grass. Who would hear them drop?"

"But why am I the only one to find them?" Rohini asked.

"Because you're there often looking for them and she's not. That's all there is to it."

Eventually, everything happened. The whole clan had become citizens, and they went to India. It was a three-week trip for Rohini and her mother, a ten-day trip for Veera, and a week's trip for Rey for the gala three-day wedding. The plan was to bring the newlyweds to the United States after their honeymoon.

Veera paid for all the trips, the engagement, the wedding, and for the newlyweds' three-day honeymoon in the island of Bali. Rohini promised to pay her brother back once she started working.

"You're not expected to pay me back, dear," Veera said with a smile. "Just listen to your husband. If he's bent on reimbursing me, do what he says, I would say, give it to a charity."

"This is something your father would have taken care of had he lived," her mother said. Her lament had become too familiar to her son and daughters. "My poor son shouldered everything just like our Lord Krishna shouldered the great mountain to safeguard the cowherds. You must have done some great penance in your previous births to have a brother like him."

Rey moved to Princeton for graduate studies in advanced math;

she had gotten a full scholarship. Rohini went to Stanford for a master's in English, which she dropped after a year to join her husband in Seattle. Veera was proud to see them pursue their interests with enthusiasm.

The twins by no means were identical. Though similar in height—they were six footers—and built—they were thin—Rohini had an oval, longish face with sharp features and Rey had a round, thin face and fair skin. To top it all off, they never saw eye to eye on anything. The fights had so far been petty—someone took the other's comb or used a sink and didn't clean it—that type of thing. Rohini would sometimes wear Rey's shirts and accessories without thinking much about it, but Rey would make a big deal of that. Rohini's logic was that all of their possessions had been bought by Veera, so sharing was fine, while Rey argued that Rohini had hers and had no right to lay a hand on Rey's.

Their first major fight seemed to be Suresh's visit. Rey could not bring herself to trust Rohini again while Rohini herself did not think it was offensive in any way and was absolutely oblivious to the effect it had on the others, especially Rey.

Rey had excused herself from attending the Columbus reception for the newlyweds blaming it on her being way out in Princeton. After Rohini's wedding, the twins' contact was minimal—once for Rohini's baby shower and another time for Veera's wedding. Their vindictiveness made them visit Veera's firstborn on different occasions, Rohini right after the birth and Rey three months later, when Veera's wife had recovered completely from childbirth. Their mother lamenting that the twins should act better for it would be just the two of them for each other when she was gone.

Their long-distance relationship could have worked had they wanted it to.

Rey completed a master's degree and started working toward a doctorate at Princeton while Rohini worked for a few months taking courses for her master's but stayed home after her first pregnancy, and she eventually had another child.

Rey met Paul at Princeton; they had a simple Hindu wedding in New York, and Veera gave them a reception at a New Jersey hotel. Rohini showed up with her family, but all three were busy—Veera with arrangements and with guests and Rohini with relatives. They separated ways right after the reception.

Rohini made sure she tipped her mother off that Rey and Paul were not tenured professors or anything big at all at Princeton and that Veera was still encumbered watching out for them.

The estranged sisters were living totally different lives. Rohini stayed home with her two little ones and managed doctors' visits and playdates. She hardly had time to be on her treadmill due to huge piles of laundry, constant grocery shopping, and trying to find time to read. There were days that Rohini did not step out of the house; she cherished going to a hair appointment or having a spa day with some ladies. Rohini's IIT husband moved to Silicon Valley, where he had always wanted to go; that rendered Rohini's job ideas insignificant and her meager income meaningless.

Rey prepared endlessly for the two classes she taught, and she spent countless hours researching for her dissertation. Paul handled the chores including cooking and shopping since his dissertation had been accepted and he did not have to spend as much time preparing for the classes he taught.

Rohini made many visits to New York City, but most of them were unknown to Rey. Their mother tried to encourage Rohini to visit Rey and Paul, but Rohini asked her mother not to let Rey know when she was near New Jersey. Rey found out about her sister's trips east after she had come and gone.

"They stayed at the Grand Marquis and saw a Broadway show," her mother would tell her. "Rohini was hauling the kids around and just couldn't make it to New Jersey."

"Mother, there's no reason for you to make excuses for her. If she wants to visit, she can. We'd be happy to accommodate them."

"Good fortune has not landed on my most genius and hard-working daughter that she languishes in a tiny apartment with no time to spare for even a phone call." As did most mothers, Rey's mother thought and prayed mostly for the one child who was not doing very well financially in her opinion.

It was actually much later that Rey learned about Rohini's visits to tarot card readers and other such soothsayers in Manhattan during her visits there with her husband and family. Her mother would sometimes mention as a conversation starter that tarot card readers had once drawn the three cards that indicated a hidden treasure in Rohini's backyard or that she was being jailed in the Grand Marquis with Rohini's children in the room while Rohini had gone out to see tarot card readers.

She had visited not one or two but several soothsayers in Manhattan all of whom had indicated in different words that Rohini would come across abundance. Rey's mother told her that she had gotten pentacles in a row at several tarot centers—the ten of pentacles, the empress surrounded by a lush oasis of a garden, a symbol of abundance! Yet another time, the nine of pentacles, a woman again in a gorgeous fertile region, and the queen of pentacles on a few other occasions, and she was again in her beautiful, bountiful nursery.

The clairvoyance had clearly predicted big harvests. Without the psychic abilities of the reader herself, the cards themselves did not say a lot, they all said. So Rohini paid them handsomely. No worries—after all, her husband was working in Silicon Valley.

One soothsayer told Rohini that there might have been a hidden treasure on her terrace or patio or in her greenhouse or yard. When Rohini got the nine of pentacles during one trip to New York, she was thoroughly convinced that she had to search the land they had built their new home on. *People everywhere in the world have come across great hidden treasures time after time, so why not me?* Rohini thought.

The wealthy and the educated gravitated to Silicon Valley at the beginning of the computer era. If that was not going to be the treasure in itself, the vast Pacific that hoarded millions literally brought them ashore as well. Treasure hunters were already there in northern California, the so-called gold country named after the state's 1849 gold rush. There was a similar rush in the early and late eighties. Big companies were there, and smaller companies cropped up everywhere. Domestic and foreign sowers were harvesting crops without worries. Motley Fool issued rare, double-up stock buy alerts every day in IPOs. High-yield dividend stocks under twenty dollars made many millionaires at least on paper. It was comical! Rohini's husband was determined not to be left out. Greediness bred like a weed. Nothing short of a filthy wealth could get them out of their bourgeois mentality.

Rohini had gone on a crusade—she dug up her yard searching for the treasure her Manhattan readers had predicted was hers for the finding. Her Silicon Valley husband did not know anything about her digging as long as it was in the far corners of their land, but soon enough, he could see what she had dug out from their kitchen window and went out to examine the holes. He bought her stories in the beginning—a flowerbed on this side, a vegetable garden on the other, and a small grove of banana trees at the edge of the land overlooking the valley in the sunniest spot. But soon enough, her feverish digging encroaching on the nearby reserve made a neighbor call the police, and he had to rush from work one morning.

After an extensive examination of the expanse, the police left around three in the afternoon, with a notice of a fine of five thousand dollars for digging up in a reserve. Rohini's story about the tarot soothsayers and her mother's idea that she was the luckiest of the three according to the star Bharani under which Rohini had been born came out slowly. Rohini firmly believed her destiny was to become a mega-rich Californian before age forty.

This and a few other incidents from the past when Rohini had indulged several of her former classmates with expensive gifts without his knowledge persuaded him to take Rohini to a counselor, who promptly diagnosed Rohini as being in an advanced stage of bipolar disorder.

When their mother called from California to get Rey's advice on the matter, she was confident and upbeat. "You see, Rey, Rohini's husband has been most supportive after the diagnosis. With some medication and counseling, he said, she should be completely okay. The highs and lows should eventually go away. He has asked Rohini to confide in him anytime, and he said she had his complete attention. Isn't that wonderful, Reva? A bad situation thwarted since it was handled appropriately. She is so lucky to have a great man for a husband. I always knew her good star would keep her like a princess, but what I didn't realize was that it would come in the form of a good man."

Rey found that laughable. "Mother, was I not born under the same star as she was being twins?"

"Oh, you're lucky too," she said patronizingly but stopped when she realized it was Rey she was conversing with. She changed the subject quickly. "Uh, one last thing, Rey. I asked Veera and Rohini's doctor that if one twin had a health issue, might the other one have it too. They said not necessarily, so you don't have to check it out for yourself."

"Mother, I'm sure I'm fine, but it won't hurt to double-check." Rey assured her that she had no problem broaching the topic with her physician.

Her mother sounded relieved when she said she had decided to stay in California with Rohini for a few more months. She added casually as though an afterthought, "And one last thing. You should come see your sister."

Rey could easily count the times she had seen her sister after the Suresh incident. "Mom, don't you worry. I'll definitely make it to see Rohini and stay for a few days with the two of you."

All is fair in love, war, and sickness.

The malady came to light two days after Rey had arrived at Rohini's palatial home.

"Rey, please don't stay in the theater room for too long or by yourself," Rohini warned her.

"Why not?"

"I'm afraid you might be watched."

"Watched? In your home? By whom?"

"Letterman."

"Letterman? David Letterman? The late-night talk-show host?"

"Exactly."

"Why would he watch me? How? From where? Hey, help me out here. I don't know where to begin asking you about this."

"I've been writing scripts and sending them to him, and guess what? I've heard him mention my topics and writings on his show. From what he says on his show, I know he's been watching me constantly. He even knows how much *&*^&* I drop in the commode every morning."

"What!?". Rey was shocked hearing the last sentence.

"In fact, take a walk with me this evening," Rohini whispered. "I'll point out the fellows who have been following me."

"Fellows following you? In this neighborhood? What are you saying?"

"I'll show you."

Rey couldn't wait for five p.m.

She walked hand in hand with Rohini to the corner. The sullenness of the nearby mountains had descended to the streets.

The quiet lane nestled charmingly under tall trees making it look like a perfect retreat in itself. The scenery down the valley and its rapturous beauty inspired anyone to relax. The entire area seemed highly exclusive and private. They didn't see a soul.

"I don't see anyone," Rey said.

"They're not here today it looks like."

Rey stood in the middle of the street looking worried. Rohini herself was agitated and in despair. After nearly a decade and a half, the twins were looking at each other in the middle of a deserted street.

"Rey, you don't trust me, right? You never have. How can I expect you after all these years to have faith in what I say?"

"Rohin, calm down. I trust you. I'm not questioning what you see. All I'm saying is, I see no one here. Be brave and take someone with you on your walks from now on. Do you promise me? The fellows may come back. I trust you."

After a week of watching her sister, Rey could only ask her mother to get all the tests done.

Rey was packing in the guest room to catch a red-eye to New Jersey with her mother beside her. Rohini was in the kitchen packing up homemade Indian snacks for Paul. Rey gathered her courage and asked her mother, "Mom, I'm no doctor or psychologist, but this is scary. Didn't I tell you about the Letterman show, the theater room, and the street-corner incidents? Get in touch with her physicians.

Nudge Rohin to vocalize all her fears. We ought to get to the bottom of this and resolve the puzzle. Don't just stand there wringing your hands, ever. Be with her all the wakeful hours when she's alone at home. Keep dispelling her delusions. Tell her there's no one watching her at all. I'll call Rohin from Jersey from now on and help dissipate her fears whenever I can. I'll have a word with Veera too. He'll know best."

"Looks like I can never run out of worries" was all her mother could say.

"Munchies for my dear nerdy brother-in-law and his equal partner," Rohini called from the stairwell. She climbed the stairs with a parcel of goodies smelling of sesame seeds, sweet jaggery, ginger, and cardamom.

Risk Mitigation

When People Shake
Their heads
Because we are
Living in a restless
Age, ask them how
They would like to
Live in a stationary
One, and do without
Change.

—George Bernard Shaw (1856–1950)

Ranjini—she went by Jinni for close friends and at work—intuited that he would be waiting in the lobby of the Cluster Office Plaza or would soon be in front of the restaurant. He had waited there for her every day the previous week. It was shocking not to mention creepy.

He had impertinently stood behind Jinni in the cocktail line as well as the food line at a party in a friend's house. It did not seem to matter to him that his wife as well as Jinni's husband were at the same party and that Jinni was also an acquaintance of his wife.

Why do I see him everywhere and every day? she wondered.

Monday lunch was busy at the second-floor cafeteria that catered to many government employees who worked in several state agencies and commissions in the Cluster Office Plaza. The office building offered several entrances to the restaurant, but an ID badge was required to get into the cafeteria. The newly renovated long verandah, atrium, and garden in front of the cafeteria were, however, open to everyone. Under the cafeteria, on the first floor, there was an atrium. Banana trees, palm trees, waterfalls and small man-made rivers and ponds sprinkled with real lilies felt like a vacation spot. Regardless of snow, ice, and rain outside, the sprawling and ornamental five-star hotel lobby atmosphere with several waterfalls offered a balmy seventy-degree respite, a quickie vacation completed with food and coffee.

Jinni had sometimes invited Melaka, who owned a small *samosa* shop in downtown Columbus, over for lunch. Since Jinni would lose her parking spot and then have to pay for one again if she went to her shop, Melaka often came over and wrote off her parking fees.

Melaka was there that day upon Jinni's request; she had packed a lunch they were going to eat in the atrium and enjoy the sight of the palm trees in beds of sand and Pebbles; There were sandwiches that Melaka had brought with *mango Lassi* and some freshly fried samosas—integral parts of all gatherings and celebrations whether they were attended by two or two hundred.

"Indian Sherlock Holmes and Dr. Watson will sleuth for roaming eyes but only after a mango lassi," Melaka said. "I'm sure your audit trips would go better if you carried some mango lassi and samosas from my store." She pulled out a glass flask and asked, "Is he here?"

"Hey, were you listening at all? If he's here, he cannot see you.

You need to surprise him. My lunch time is usually twelve thirty to one thirty. I'm sure he'll be here shortly."

"Are you sure he's looking for you? I mean, Cluster Office has too many Indian guys and gals working in their IT, actuarial, and even HR departments. He may be looking for someone else."

"Every day?"

"He's been here every day?"

"Every day last week."

"Was he attending meetings and conferences here? Isn't he an IT guy?"

"People leave after meetings or conferences. They don't hang out in the lobby, especially on weekdays."

"Let's first be sure of your theory. Tell me again about the last few parties where you and the harasser, I mean, the man who's driving you up the wall, were present. What were you wearing?" Melaka asked with a laugh.

"Be serious, Melaka."

"Agreed."

"Do I look easy?"

"You could be vain and shallow at a party, but easy? Absolutely not."

The women were in their mid-forties and married; their children were growing up.

"My peeve is that you're not taking this in."

"My apologies. Jokes apart, please run this by me again, Jinni.

I'll buy into this when I'm thoroughly convinced. He is after all my cousin's hubby."

"Okay, here it is. Your cousin's hubby has been eyeing me in parties and other Indian gatherings in a way I don't like. I've ignored him. I thought he was just going through a midlife crisis or something. But I've been seeing him every day here, which made me think he knows someone here in the Cluster Office building. I know he doesn't work here. I thought that even if he were here looking for me, if I didn't give him any encouragement, he'd get bored and try following someone else."

Jinni paused.

"I hear a 'but' coming, Jinni."

"A big one. At our last get-together, my husband or maybe I—I don't remember—may have inadvertently blurted out something about my audit trips. I went to Ironton in Lawrence County, one of the most downtrodden places in Ohio I've ever had to go to audit, and that place has only one hotel. I got there about five thirty and saw him waiting, or should I say sitting on a couch in the lobby reading something."

"My goodness! Seriously?"

"Yes. I was there just two days. I'd see him in the mornings at breakfast and in the evening when I got back to the hotel. I had colleagues with me on all occasions. We finished our work early and got back to Columbus. I could have thought his being there was a coincidence, but Ironton? It has nothing that would draw an IT guy. The place has no big businesses. And then last week, I saw him here, in my office building every single day. That's creepy. His kids are my kids' ages, and they're all friends. This has to stop before something bad happens."

"Let's go with the idea he had work in Ironton and that being the only hotel there and all. Add to it that he was here in the Cluster Office building for work too."

"Yes, but just hear me out, Melaka. Last Saturday, around six thirty, I was walking my dog when I saw a metallic-blue Acura driving toward me. The driver saw me, stopped far before I could reach him, drove into a neighbor's driveway, turned around, and sped away. Or at least I thought he did. But farther down, I saw whoever it was parked at a grassy knoll at the entrance to our subdivision. I was sure he saw me. I've seen your cousin come to your place in a shiny blue car. I recognized him as I got closer. He didn't come to your place, neither did he knock on my door. He was just waiting there. I turned around and came home. I have no idea how long he stayed there. Don't know what the idea is behind all this—just drive around, see, and leave?"

Mally was somber. "Yes, they own a blue car, an Acura I think."

They were silent for a bit.

Mally asked, "So what's the plan?"

"Don't know, Mally."

Jinni called her Mally when she felt the closest to her or when she felt vulnerable. "RBIA—risk-based internal auditing—tells you to straighten the accounts based on past actions and perceived risks and strike while the iron is hot. Don't they say, 'The saddest truth is that people believe the worst rumors about a woman while they'll gladly ignore the worst facts about a man.' It's always the woman who bears the cross. She must have done something, been too loose, has no restraint, and so on."

"I don't doubt that."

"Let me remind you about your friend Leena who kept badgering you about a call coming from your home number to her husband's office number".

"Yes, she adamantly believed I was the one calling her husband. It turned out that my brother who was visiting me called Leena's husband, but my brother did not leave any messages".

"Yes, but do you remember the worst part? Leena's husband informed Leena that you were calling him because he checked with your hubby who said he did not make any calls to their home".

"The self-touting imagination of some men! They are the saviors of the damsel in distress, I was in some wanton need and he was my womanhood's knight in shining armor."

"Do you see how I could be the victim? Our own women would affirm it's the girl who should have behaved."

"Forget it."

"Again, Mally, you know how this might go. If someone sees him here looking at me or following me, somehow, they'll make me the villain—I just know. The victim will be victimized easily, and I'm sure he knows that. He knows he can get off scot-free in situations like this. And we have enemies in our circle for good reasons. Before it gets blown out of proportions, I want to nip it in the bud."

"I'd love to kick this fellow in the groin. Let's do it right now—no explanations. You know I was just teasing. What's the plan?"

"I thought that if you saw him here, said hello to him, and told him you're going to be with me to get some auditing tips for your own business, he might back off since he and you are from the same village in India and speak the same language. You know his folks, his parents and sister very well, with his wife being your first cousin and everything. He won't jeopardize his life when people he knows too well were watching.

"This is just a fling like I said, a midlife crisis. Some men buy fancy cars, and some are hypnotized by affairs. Maybe it's become fashionable to have affairs? You and I are probably too old to understand this. Easier too when you're married. Something new to experiment with, like, moving from margaritas to cocktails."

"What do you mean by 'easier when married'?"

"Experienced. The teabag is actually better the second time around."

"No double entendre now. Or it may be that your retirement

package that he is after which is better than his with your being a government employee and all."

"Wow, how romantic! Thank you. What am I thinking, uh? Here I am, being all high about my looks at late forties voluptuous enough that someone could be smitten with me?" She laughed.

"Sorry to burst your luscious bubble."

They both now laughed heartily.

"Jokes aside, this could become a problem if left unchecked. With an early intervention, this might become null and void and affect no one. I came up with this because I know you'll keep it to yourself. Can this live and die with these two besties?" Jinni pointed at herself and Melaka in turns.

"Fair enough. We're BFFs. It's worth trying."

"Let's wait here hidden by the palm trees. I know where he's stood every day for the past week. I'll take the escalator up and see if he's standing there. If so, I'll text you. You can come up and watch him as I head toward the cafeteria. I'm sure that his eyes will be following me and that he won't be expecting you. So, you come up behind him, call his name out, and act surprised that you had seen him there. You shake hands and start asking him questions right away. Don't waste time exchanging pleasantries. That might give him time to think. Say something right away like, 'Hey! I didn't know you worked here.' And don't forget to say you're here to have lunch with me. Just be natural. If he says he's visiting a friend, ask him if you know him, if he works here. Ask about his wife and kids later. Watch him for any uneasiness, clues—anything. Remember what he says—take mental notes on everything so you can relate it all to me."

"I'll also tell him I come here often to have lunch with you and have been here many times."

"Yes exactly. Just don't give him much time to think, and note his body language, his comfort level in seeing you. You're a shrewd businesswoman, Melaka. You can see through things. I want to scare him. He doesn't know that you and I are very close. You don't have a Facebook account, but I know he watches me on Facebook daily. He sent a friend request that I just ignored. If you can shake him, I'm sure he'll stop this nonsense. If this doesn't work, I'll have to try something else."

"Okay, but let's try this first."

Just then Jinni saw him staring at the escalator leading up from the atrium at twelve thirty-five.

"I just saw him. Rubber meets the road. I'll take the escalator up and confirm. Wait at the handrail and get on the escalator some ten steps behind me. Good luck."

They got up from the cozy wooden bench, walked out of the man-made oasis, and hid behind the palm trees for a minute. Jinni approached the escalator and got on it. Melaka waited for some people to get on the escalator in front of her, so she could ascend inconspicuously.

Jinni reached the landing and walked toward the restaurant swipe gates. She made sure it was in fact him; she texted Melaka.

Melaka came up and saw him following Jinni. She took a few steps in his direction and quickly caught up with him from behind. She said in a loud voice, "Oh look who's here!" She sounded excited and dramatic as well as loud.

He turned around on hearing her familiar voice and without controlling his surprise asked, "Hey! What are you doing here?"

"A luncheon meeting with Ranjini, you know, my auditor friend. She works in this building. How about you? You work here?"

The short drama ended with his hurriedly saying he was leaving after meeting a friend. He turned around and took the escalator down.

After making sure that he had left the building, Mally joined Jinni at the other end of the long corridor.

"You did it, Jinni. Looks like he was following you. He was visibly upset and agitated when he saw me. He left in a hurry. I watched him until he pushed through the revolving door and exited on High Street."

"I don't think he'll be back tomorrow or ever, but would you indulge me in this for a couple of more days just in case?"

"Will do," Mally said with a little sadness.

"Thinking of your cousin?"

"Yes. She's sweet and quite the helpful type."

"The things we do to keep our little freedom and not hurt others in the process, huh?"

"It would be humiliating if our husbands tried something like that—trying to hook up with someone or start a serious affair that could end up in a divorce."

"Yes, but unfortunately, this is how it starts."

"But Jinni, tell me one thing. If this had been someone you liked, would you have gone along with it?"

"The answer is an easy 'no'. I am no family-wrecker. Unless it was the dead bard himself from London, no." She tried to be funny with the last sentence.

"Oh, c'mon. If this had been someone awesome, an amazing man, would you have gone along with it?"

"Good question. It's not that complicated if one has a decent sense of right and wrong. Of course, a lot depends on how your life and marriage are at that point."

"Mynah says men with a daughter will not have affairs."

"That's idiotic bull-@#^%. That's one of the excuses some Indian women give to justify their own husband's proliferation."

"Proliferation? Really? Nuclear proliferation?" Maleka sounded irate. She wanted Jinni to be wrong about her cousin's husband; Jinni understood her disappointment; knew where the satire came from.

"Mally, I know, I'm sorry—also, my plot is tepid, but it's good enough for now."

"We shouldn't be required to do this from our teen to our twilight years."

"Exactly."

"But he looks like he'll find someone else if not you."

"So, you are agreeing with me that he tried me albeit this may just be a fling. He is bored in his middle age and wants some excitement?"

"which will eventually lead to adultery which is a bombshell. It's akin to abuse."

"I think all men and women who are in a relationship, it be a marriage or partnership, should have a robust full life outside of the marriage – in work or a passion or something useful to society. So even if betrayal happens, its sting will not be that painful. You may not get burned too much."

"A broken-heart mended by a busy life?" dry chuckle ensued from Mally.

"I'm no feminist or a martyr sacrificing her life for this wonderful system called marriage if it was bad, but the institution named family is way too precious though we do not discuss this topic often and mostly take it for granted."

Mally came around to have lunch with Jinni for the entire week. They did not see him in his usual spot until Friday. He was looking up the escalator on that day at twelve thirty-five. They saw his head for a few seconds, and then he was gone. The two middle-aged women ran up the escalator together but could not find him up there or anywhere down the entire corridor. He had absconded!

CPSIA information can be obtained
at www.ICGtesting.com
Printed in the USA
LVHW040811021219
639121LV00002B/133/P